COWBOYS DON'T HAVE A SECRET BABY

First edition. April 23, 2019.

Copyright © 2019 Jessie Gussman.

Written by Jessie Gussman.

D1521880

Cover art by Brenda Walter https://bluevalleyauthorservices.site/

Editing by Heather Hayden https://hhaydeneditor.com/

Narration by Jay Dyess https://www.acx.com/narrator?p=A3VWKVSC6MFZHW

Click HERE[1] if you'd like to subscribe to my newsletter and find out why people say "Jessie's is the only newsletter I open and read." And "You make my day brighter. Love, love, love reading your newsletters. I don't know where you find time to write books. You are so busy living life. A true blessing." And "I know from now on that I can't be drinking my morning coffee while reading your newsletter – I laughed so hard I sprayed it out all over the table!"

---

1.   https://BookHip.com/FASFD

Dedication: to my second son

My second son was so easy to raise. Don't you love those kids that make you look like a good parent? He did anything I asked. He excelled in school. He plays the piano in church. He also played both the violin and viola in the homeschool orchestra. He took the money he made delivering papers and bought all the equipment to reload his own rifle and shotgun shells, a complicated process that requires precision and patience. One time our insurance man was visiting and took a fifty-cent piece up to the pasture field. I could barely see it from the porch, but my son took his rifle and shot a hole through the center of it. He's part-owner of our trucking company and the head mechanic. He can tear down and rebuild a big CAT engine, and several of our trucks are working every day with motors he built. Plus, he's a genuine nice guy. I love you, Boo.

Chapter 1

"We're leaving in fifteen minutes."

Ty Hanson pulled the covers over his head and rolled over. It was a juvenile thing to do, of course. And it wouldn't get him out of going to church. Never had. Maybe he was twenty-eight years old and the highest paid forward in the NHL, but his mother didn't relax her rules just because he was famous. If you were in her house on Sunday morning, you went to church with the family.

Ty snorted as he threw the covers off and pulled his feet from where they hung over the end of the too-small bed, setting them firmly on the floor. It wouldn't take him that long to get ready. His appearance, anyway. He'd probably never be fully ready to show his face at the Sweet Water Baptist Church again.

A knock sounded on his door. "Did you hear me?" his mother asked.

"I'm up. I don't have any dress clothes."

"What you wore to the reception will be fine."

A wave of heat followed by a chill washed over him. He wasn't going to think about the wedding.

Actually, it had probably been a nice wedding. Simple. Quick. Lots of good food. Didn't get much better than that. He'd shown up late, though, and arrived after the ceremony. That's when the problem occurred, while he was holding his plate and mingling with townsfolk that he hadn't seen in years. He caught a glimpse of the skeleton in his closet.

She was beautiful.

She was with someone. Someone who probably suited her much better than he ever had. Ty could have easily broken that man apart

3

with his bare hands. The fellow was skinny. His glasses perched on the end of his nose, and his suit didn't quite fit. Strands of gray ran through his slightly balding head, and the entire time Ty watched, the guy didn't shut up.

Louise Olson had hung on his every word. Like she'd hung on Ty's, one summer long ago.

Ty yanked the covers up, making the bed in one sweep, and pulled his jeans off the chair he'd hung them on the day before when he'd come in from another hard day of work. Depressed.

It served him right. He'd left her. And he hadn't come back.

He had the plaid button-down on and tucked in before he walked out through the living room and into the small kitchen. In North Dakota, the winters were long and cold, and a small house was easier to heat. His parents had raised three kids in this tiny place. Despite the cold, they hadn't spent much time in the house anyway. There was always work to do on the ranch, and once it got cold enough, he and his older brother, Ford, spent all their free time ice-skating on the pond behind the barn.

Georgia, their sister, had tagged along too. He'd seen Georgia at the wedding, but Ford hadn't come. Unsurprisingly. If he wanted to see Ford, he'd need to drive out to the ranch Ford bought a few years ago. If Ford had left the ranch once he moved in, Ty didn't know about it.

There were a lot of things that Ty didn't know.

Like who the man was that Louise had been with. And why he even cared, since he hadn't seen her in almost nine years.

"Good morning," his mother greeted him from the kitchen table where she sat with a half-eaten piece of toast on her plate and a steaming mug of coffee in front of her.

"'Morning, Mom. You make two cups?" he asked, nodding at her coffee.

"Of course." She gave him a gentle smile.

Why hadn't he come home? The thought ran through his mind until he opened the cupboard and saw his dad's old coffee cup perched on the edge. It'd been almost a decade since the funeral and a stupid coffee cup could still make his chest hurt and his throat tighten.

In order to not have to touch it, he picked up the pink one on the second shelf. His sister's old cup. His was probably in there somewhere, but he wasn't moving his dad's to look for it.

"You're not limping as bad today." His mother's hair had turned gray years ago, but her blue eyes were still sparkling and young. She could have remarried.

"It's not hurting as bad."

"It's funny how rough those hockey games look on TV, yet you get injured jogging in the park."

"Yeah." He didn't want to talk about tearing the ligaments in his leg. They'd be healed by the time the season started. It's what the surgeon had said anyway. His agent was the one that demanded he go home.

He poured coffee in the cup and carried it to the table. His mother eyed the pink but didn't say anything, although a tiny worry line appeared between her brows. She'd kept her mouth closed over the years, never pressuring him to come home. Occasionally she'd hinted around, digging for info about any relationships. Maybe she'd read rumors about him. There were plenty of those.

"It was the closest one." He lifted the pink cup.

His mother, with her white skin that flushed easily, ice-blue eyes, and hair that had been blond before it turned gray, was Norwegian through and through. Hardworking, thrifty, and stoic. Just like their ancestors who had settled this land and made a living in a country that was so like their homeland.

Still, he couldn't miss her concern. But she didn't have to worry; he would never disappoint his mother that way. "Honest, Mom. The pink cup was closest, and I'm going to make you late."

She smiled a little, still beautiful in her fifties. "I'm thrilled that you're here."

He hid his own smile. This was about as thrilled as her Norwegian ancestry would allow her to be, calmly sitting at the kitchen table, sipping coffee while her son who'd barely been home for more than a day at a time in nine years sat down with her. Even in Pittsburgh, where he lived, the German and English with their stiff upper lips couldn't compare to the emotionless Norwegians of his childhood.

"I'm thrilled to be here," he said, allowing his lips to turn up.

His mother saw, and her own face brightened some. "Still making fun of me."

"Mom, when someone is 'thrilled,' they do more than sip their coffee."

"I would have cooked you breakfast if you'd come down earlier. There's not time, now."

He laughed outright. The guys he played with might not be entirely in touch with their emotional side, but they knew how to do "thrilled" with shouts and slaps and fist pumps. Not a tiny smile and a sip of coffee and an offer to cook breakfast.

Sometimes still waters ran deep.

Louise had blue eyes too, a shade lighter even than his mom's. Her studious exterior had hidden a wealth of emotion, hot and powerful.

He shook the image. That ship had sailed, even if she was still the standard by which he judged every single female that came into his orbit.

"I don't eat in the morning, anyway."

"Your father never did either. Not until the stock was fed."

He clenched his jaw, determined she not see that he'd never gotten over his dad's death. Probably because of the way they'd ended.

"I know. I was with him." All through his childhood, Ford and he were his dad's shadows.

Her expression was benevolent, and he was sure she was remembering the happier days when his dad was alive. Back when they were the perfect ranching family. Before Ford's accident when he and his brother were high school sports stars that spent their spare time on the farm, working and playing. He couldn't have had a better childhood. Then Ford got hurt. And not long after that, he and his dad had had the first fight of their lives.

That night, his dad had died.

He hadn't been home to help on the worst night of his mom's life. Hadn't gotten to apologize to his dad or race him to the hospital.

He'd been with Louise.

The drive to church wasn't long. Only about twenty minutes to the east. His mom rode in the passenger seat of his rented car, her gelatin salad held on her lap, the hot dish on the seat in the back. He wished they could have driven separately, because she would want to stay and eat and talk, and he didn't, not after the trouble he'd had at the wedding. It wasn't because of people recognizing him and wanting his autograph, although they had, to some extent, but Sweet Water was just as Norwegian as his mother, and they'd been very polite about it.

No, the trouble had been when he'd seen Louise.

He pulled into the gravel lot, beside the small, white church of his childhood, the August heat making the car's AC feel necessary. The lot was already full, and they parked way back.

"I'll carry these things in," he said as he got out. He hadn't seen Louise in the week since the wedding. Of course, he'd been at the house a lot, since he'd been doing a lot of repair work for his mother who was hoping to sell the ranch. This week, she'd be away at a craft fair, and he'd be getting out more.

"You'll have to put the salad in the fridge. The Acapulco Chicken should be fine. It's insulated."

"Okay." He headed toward the back door, while his mother went in the front. The service would be starting soon. It was funny that he didn't hear any music. He'd always enjoyed the simple piano music and hymns in his home church.

By the time he had the food situated and crept up the stairs to the back of the sanctuary, Pastor Houpe was talking. Still no music. Odd.

Their family's pew was clear at the front, and he went up the side aisle as inconspicuously as a guy as big as he was could before slipping in beside his mother. He'd have sat in the back, but she was alone at the front. He'd never considered that she might sit by herself on Sunday mornings. Ford and Georgia weren't that far away. Forty-five minutes. Maybe they went to a different church.

He settled in the seat, resting his arm on the back of the pew behind his mother.

The preacher's next words were, "We're happy to have Titus Hanson here today."

Figures. He was used to attention, and it didn't really bother him.

"Not as happy as Mrs. Hanson, I'm sure," Pastor Houpe continued.

His mother clutched her Bible. She wasn't used to the attention, and he was sure it did bother her.

"How long is he here for, Mrs. Hanson?" the pastor asked.

Ty had forgotten how relaxed the services in his small country church actually were. This would never happen in Pittsburgh.

"A month," his mother said in a confident tone. She didn't like the attention, but his mother never backed down from anything. Pride stirred in his chest.

"That's great. We look forward to getting to know you again, Ty."

Ty nodded in acknowledgement, and the pastor spoke again. "Let's move on to the morning's announcements. Our pianist is home with her daughter who is under the weather. We'll put her on the prayer list. In the meantime, we'll sing without a piano today." He shuffled the papers on the pulpit. "Ladies' Missionary Group meets Thursday night." He looked out over the congregation. "See Patty back there in the last row for the location and time." People shifted as they looked around at Patty.

Ty was pretty sure she was the daughter of Claudette who used to own the diner that was now called Patty's Diner. It was still open. He'd noticed that when they'd driven down the street. The C Store was still there, too, as well as the hardware store and the butcher shop. There were still two bars, but it looked like the third one had been turned into a gym. The one right across the street from Patty's Diner. He hadn't known, but it would save him a lot of time driving to the next town over for his workouts.

"Palmer and Ames gave me this to read to you." The pastor waved a card in the air before holding it in front of his face and reading. "'We appreciate everyone who came to our wedding and especially those who helped out. We'll be back next week to open gifts. Love, Palmer and Ames Hanson.'"

The pastor looked up. "It was a nice wedding. 'Course, they're back from their honeymoon now and with us this morning."

Ty had to agree that the wedding had been nice. Simple and quick. Not formal. Just a down-home feel where everyone had a great time.

"Thanks," a deep voice said from behind him. He didn't twist all the way around, but he assumed it was Palmer. He'd known both Palmer and Ames from high school. They'd all gotten along fine. Of course, Palmer might have a few choice things to say to him if he knew that Ty had been meeting his sister down by the river the summer before he left. Actually, he probably wouldn't mind the meeting. It was the other things they'd done that would land him in a fistfight with Louise's brother.

"The men's prayer breakfast is on Saturday morning. We'll meet out at the pavilion at seven. And..." The pastor gathered all the papers and tapped them on the pulpit. "We need volunteers for the Harvest Fest committee."

The church was silent.

"I volunteer the pianist," a voice said from the other side of the room.

Titters sounded from the pews. The pastor grinned with good nature. "I guess if you don't want to be volunteered, you need to show up and say so."

"She'll do it," an older lady said from somewhere close behind Ty. Again, he didn't turn around.

"Thanks, Grandma Gene. I'll put her down." The pastor wrote a note on the papers. "I need a co-chair."

Silence reigned again.

His mother's hand landed softly, like a butterfly, on his leg. Ty knew the question she was asking. He waited another five beats of silence, hoping someone else would speak up. He'd be heading back to Pittsburgh and training camp about that time.

"What all does it entail?" a nasally voice asked from across the aisle. Ty turned his head, his height making it easy to see over the heads between. He recognized the man who'd been talking to Louise at the wedding yesterday.

His mother's hand ran smack into his competitive streak. The explosion in his chest was inevitable. He might not be competing for Louise. He'd thrown that right away. She might even be married to the dude for all he knew. She wasn't beside him. He hadn't seen her at all the few times he'd looked around.

But she'd been talking to this guy at the reception last Sunday afternoon the short moment he'd seen her. His crazy brain latched onto him as the competition to beat. Never mind that the person who got stuck planning Harvest Fest was actually the loser.

"I'll do it," he said, loud and clear before the pastor had a chance to explain what the job entailed.

All eyes shifted to him. He was used to being in the spotlight. On the ice and off it. But it was hard because this was his community and he'd left. Still, so far, they'd not seemed to hold it against him.

The pastor wasted no time. He was writing his name beside the hapless pianist's before Ty's mouth was even closed. Ty felt a bit like he'd been hooked. "Okay then. You two will need to get together, but I'll let you handle that."

His mom would know who the pianist was. She'd have the number too. Ty pictured himself working with an eighty-year-old woman. Mrs. Hoyt, the pianist of his childhood, had passed to her reward years ago. He remembered his mother telling him. So he wouldn't know the new one.

It would require no brainpower from him. He'd be the strong legs and back that carried out all her plans. As long as his leg held up, he was good with that. Hopefully she'd be a good cook, because right here, where he came from, old women who could cook usually rewarded the strong legs and back with good food.

LOUISE WATCHED THE dust cloud in the distance. It was almost certainly her family coming home. She stroked Tella's hair. Her daughter had fallen asleep on the porch swing a while ago. At the ripe old age of eight, she'd decided she was too big to take a nap in the afternoon, no matter that she had a fever.

A little shot of fear went through Louise. Sicknesses were definitely one of the times she wished she had a husband. Should she make the one-hour trip to the clinic in the next town? Or was it just a harmless summer virus that would be gone when Tella woke up from her nap?

Hoping it was the latter, she continued to stroke the soft golden hair. Just like her father's. She'd inherited his deep blue eyes too. Eyes that looked like the first blueberries of the season kissed with summer dew. Eyes Louise had gotten lost in back when she was young and dumb as dirt.

He'd come home. After nine years, Ty Hanson had come back to Sweet Water. He'd been at Palmer and Ames's reception last Sunday afternoon, although Louise hadn't seen him in the church for the actual wedding. Didn't mean he wasn't there. She'd been busy.

But he'd been at the reception. No missing him. He was the biggest guy in the churchyard. In height and if one were counting muscle mass, he'd win that contest too. Not that that meant anything to her. It didn't. She appreciated Paul's intellectual prowess. He was an IT consultant. He had his own business and did most of his work online. And, yes, he indulged in the occasional Friday night at the bar. Okay.

But, really, what else was there to do in Sweet Water for a middle-aged, unmarried man?

And who else was there for her to make a bargain with? To provide her daughter with the father she was lacking?

Thoughts of the letter she'd received a month ago pushed sharp twinges of anxiety up her spine as they always did. As a single mom, her focus had always been on what was best for her daughter. From giving up college to staying on the ranch she'd grown up on to raise her daughter the same way, to getting a job at the diner. Everything was for Tella.

So why hadn't she gone through with the deal she'd offered Paul? The letter had said if she got married and settled in North Dakota, anywhere in North Dakota, she'd inherit one billion dollars. As a single mother, with the welfare of her daughter always first and foremost, she should be jumping all over that offer. A father and enough money to buy her own ranch. Perfect.

At first, she'd thought the letter was some kind of joke. Then she found out that her brother Palmer had gotten the same offer. He'd gone to the lawyer who'd sent it and checked it out. The owner of Sweet Water Ranch had indeed left a billion dollars to Palmer. He'd had to get married as well. And he had. Just last Sunday. They'd been gone on their honeymoon, but they'd been able to draw on the money before the actual marriage.

Palmer didn't know about her letter, and she hadn't told him. Her grandparents who lived with them didn't know either. Maybe some people would tell everyone, but Louise kept the information close. Her family would never want her to marry for money. Yet the chances of her falling in love again were zero. She'd given her heart once. Ty hadn't taken very good care of it.

The one billion dollars Palmer would get was more than enough to pay the medical bills from Pap's stroke and get him top-of-the-line medical care. So the ranch was out of financial trouble and on the way to being a profitable family venture again.

Unfortunately, as nice as Ames was, Louise had started to feel like a third leg on a chicken. Palmer and Ames had only been back from their short honeymoon for a few days—they were taking a longer honeymoon later in the fall when the harvest was over—and Ames had been nothing but kindness and sweetness to Louise and Tella. But it had to be awkward stepping over her sister-in-law and her daughter every day.

The big, old farmhouse had been built with no concern about heat on a cold winter day, so there was plenty of room. And Gram and Pap lived downstairs, anyway.

Palmer would never think of leaving, and Ames probably wouldn't ask. So it was up to Louise to move out.

Not that she wanted to. She loved ranch life. Cooking and baking and canning. Feeding the animals and riding the fence line. Tella had her own horse and free range of the wide outdoors.

Tella stirred on the swing. Louise put her hand on her forehead. Still warm. But not hot. Thankfully. Tella sighed and sat up slowly, looking around, trying to get her bearings.

"You fell asleep on the swing."

"I never sleep during the day," Tella said groggily. Her daughter might be eight, but she had so many adults in her life that she acted and spoke more like a miniature adult than a child.

"You did today."

Tella, one side of her face streaked red where it had lain on Louise's lap, gave her a sour look. "I didn't want to sleep."

"Sometimes your body needs rest to heal. You're not as hot as you were."

"I feel better. Will you take me swimming?"

Louise wanted to laugh and roll her eyes at the same time. A father would keep her from being the bad guy all the time, too. Ideally. "No. I want to make sure you're completely better before we go swimming."

"But you were busy with the ranch this past week and didn't have time. And next week, you'll be working again. Then school starts."

Louise pressed her lips together and watched as the car parked. Palmer drove with Ames beside him. Gram and Pap were in the back.

She had been busy this past week with Palmer gone most of it, even though she'd taken a vacation from her waitressing job at the diner.

She didn't do any fieldwork, but she'd taken care of all of the stock plus tried to keep up with the garden and canning. Truth be told, she'd been a little happy Tella was sick. She hated seeing her daughter ill, but she was exhausted and appreciated the break from church.

Okay, she was a coward. She didn't know how long Ty would be in town, but she didn't want to see him, either. She'd dreaded the idea that she might run into him today. His mother didn't recognize the dark blue eyes and light brown hair of her grandchild or the telling cleft in her chin. It was so much like Ty's it pulled a reaction out of Louise's gut every time she looked at her daughter's face. But Ty's mother, Donna, hadn't ever seemed to notice. Would Ty?

Louise assumed Donna would have no reason to look at Louise's child and wonder if it were Ty's. Louise and Ty had never even been friends, let alone a couple. All their meetings that summer had been clandestine ones by the river. But Ty would know. Or maybe, with his sports star life and puck bunny bedmates, he'd not remember.

As much as the last idea pained her heart, drat the stupid thing anyway, it would be for the best if he didn't remember. She had never told anyone who Tella's father was. Partly because she was embarrassed of her own stupidity, and she didn't need the whole town laughing at her too, but partly because she didn't want anyone pulling Ty out of his college scholarship and demanding he quit hockey to support a daughter he didn't want. Or worse, demanding he marry her.

She bit her lip and pushed her thoughts away. Rising from the swing, she walked down the steps and walk and took Gram's arm as she got out of the car. Palmer and Ames walked on either side of Pap.

"How's Tella?" Gram asked.

"She's better. Not as warm, but I think she still has a fever."

"Good. That's the way those summer viruses usually go."

"Yeah, I remember her getting them when she was little, but it's been a few years since she's been sick in the summer."

Gram patted her hand where it rested on the inside of her bent elbow. "That's the way it goes. Life happens, and we forget."

Unless one happened to be forced to look into dark blue eyes shining out from a face that called her "mommy" every day. Then one couldn't forget. Even if they wanted to.

"Lou Lou." Palmer's voice came behind her with the old nickname he and Sawyer used on her growing up. "Guess what you got volunteered for today?"

She grunted. It couldn't be any worse than the last time she'd missed church, a year and a half ago at Christmas time. She'd been volunteered to be Mary in the church's live nativity. It wouldn't have been too bad, but Paul had been Joseph, and it had been one of the coldest Christmas weeks on record. Paul had flaked out. Louise had ended up by the manger alone, fitting for a single mother, she supposed, dressed in coveralls and three layers of clothes underneath her blue robe. There were probably other "Marys" in North Dakota that year, and other years, too, who wore beanie hats under their head coverings and had gloves and insulated boots on under their robes. But she doubted any of them knelt at the manger alone.

When Palmer had gotten done feeding the stock and come in town, he'd thrown Joseph's robe on and knelt with her. Bless him. Even if he was annoying.

And still waiting for her to guess what she'd been volunteered for this time.

She kept a good grip on Gram's arm. "I have no idea. Hopefully they haven't decided to exhume anyone."

"Ew. I wouldn't let them volunteer you for that," Ames said.

"I would," Palmer replied, even though no one had asked him.

"I know you would. And Ames can't watch you every second." Louise steadied Gram as she took one porch step at a time. There were five steps. Gram and Louise had done this a lot together. Before that, she'd lugged baby carriers, buggies, and then a little girl up and down so many times she had all the dips and creaks memorized. She'd fallen down them once while carrying Tella as a baby. Thankfully she was able to catch herself on knees and elbows—she still had the scars—and Tella had survived unscathed. She hadn't even woken up.

"I didn't volunteer you for this, though," Palmer said from behind her, where Pap was waiting to come up the steps behind them. One of the things Palmer was going to do with his money was install a ramp.

"Who did?"

"Not sure. But I did agree when Pastor laughed and said you wouldn't mind."

"Just tell me." Louise figured it couldn't be too bad, since he was laughing. Of course, if she'd been volunteered to replace the church roof, Palmer would think that was funny too.

"You're co-chairing the Harvest Fest committee," Ames said.

Gram made it to the top, and Tella moved silently to open the door for her. To Louise's eyes, Tella still moved a little stiffly, but that could be because of sleeping on the swing. There was no cushion.

"That's fine. I can do that." She'd never chaired Harvest Fest, but she'd pulled her weight in every single one of the festivals the town had. She could handle doing Harvest Fest, one of the biggest.

"Paul almost volunteered to do it with you." Gram hobbled through the open door, giving Louise a look she couldn't decipher. Louise stood at the door and waited for Pap to come up with Ames and Palmer.

"But he didn't?" Louise asked, hoping the answer was no. Sure, she was considering marrying him, but under a "deal" type of arrangement and only so Tella had a father and for Louise to get money to buy their own ranch. They weren't pretending to be in love.

"Nope," Palmer said with a smirk. "Paul was hemming and hawing around about how much work it was going to be and what was involved."

That totally sounded like Paul. With his IT background, he wanted to gather all the facts and analyze the situation. He was just like Louise in that regard. The one time in her life she'd closed her eyes and jumped, she'd had a crash landing. Tella was the only good thing to rise from the ashes of that big mistake.

"And Ty Hanson, who was sitting with his mother right in front of us, jumped in before Paul could stumble out any more irritating questions and volunteered for the spot." Palmer laughed like Ty one-upping Paul was funny.

Palmer and Ames were just helping Pap up the last step, so when the screen door banged shut the way no one was allowed to ever let happen, they both looked up with wide eyes.

The porch floor seemed to move under Louise's feet.

"Are you okay?" Ames asked, the sound of her voice seeming to come from a distance away.

Louise reminded herself to breathe. In and out. In and out.

Ty was here, and he was apparently staying for at least a month or so. Long enough to be here until Harvest Fest. The Harvest Fest that she was going to plan. With him.

There weren't too many times in Louise's life where she cried out to the Lord in protest at the unfairness of life. Most of the bad things that had happened to her were clearly her own fault. Or, like her parents not really wanting their children, the bumps in life that one had to weather. But this? After all she'd been through, God was going to make her do this?

She was going to drive in this afternoon and tell Pastor she couldn't, wouldn't co-chair with him. She wouldn't mention his name, but she'd be very clear. She wasn't doing Harvest Fest with Ty Hanson.

"Mom? Are you getting the door?"

Tella stood beside her, looking up with her brows puckered.

Louise shook herself. "I think I might have a touch of what Tella had earlier. I'm going to go lie down." Without looking at anyone else, she opened the screen door and walked in.

It wasn't often that she had been allowed the luxury of pouting in her room all day. She didn't usually allow herself to mope. What good did it do?

But for several hours on Sunday afternoon, she gave in to her inner child and lay on her bed staring at the ceiling as the sun moved across the sky, the lace pattern shadow of her curtain creeping along the floor.

Memories of a summer long ago slipped through her mind. Good memories. Even the last. Ty had promised to call. He'd sworn he'd visit as much as he could. Maybe every weekend. He'd even offered to take her with him, although how they were going to work that out with her having another year of school, he didn't say.

Yet, he'd left, and she'd never heard another word. Not one.

Of course, his father had died. He'd stayed long enough for the funeral. He hadn't gone to the river to meet her, although she'd waited there every night. But she'd understood, or at least thought she did. He had family in and couldn't get away. Until he left, the day after the funeral, without talking to her again.

She'd been pregnant her whole senior year. Her graduation gown might have hidden her huge belly, but Tella had been born the night Louise was scheduled to give her valedictorian's speech. It had been a hard year. A lot of judgment in their small, religious town. A lot of disappointment in her family and herself. She persevered. Then she missed the day that was supposed to validate it all: her graduation.

She didn't know where Ty was, but he hadn't come home.

Maybe because of her recent grief, maybe because of how her family had splintered, but Ty's mother, Donna, had attached herself to Tella. Officially, on the birth certificate, her name was Donatella, but no one knew that. Still, Miss Donna had fallen in love with Louise's baby at church. She'd kept her in the nursery, then she'd offered to watch her when Louise started waitressing at Patty's.

Louise didn't have her do it every day, but Miss Donna had almost taken over her rightful role as grandmother. As far as Louise knew, Miss Donna had no idea she was watching her grandchild.

Still, Ty hadn't come home. At least not to see her.

Why now? People had talked about his poor mother and how she lost her husband and about Ford's accident and how the whole family had seemed to fall apart, with Ty never coming home on his breaks or even after graduation, Ford becoming a recluse in a town forty-five minutes away, and Georgia moving in to take care of Ford.

Why had he volunteered to co-chair with her? What was going on?

The room had darkened, and she couldn't dwell on Ty's motivations. Maybe he volunteered first. She tried to remember exactly what Palmer and Ames had said but couldn't be sure from her memories whether her name had been suggested first or not.

Her bigger concerns were why did he have to come back and what was she going to do?

Funny, last time he was here, she hadn't wanted him to disappear forever.

This time, her dearest wish was that he would leave and never come back.

Chapter 2

Monday morning at seven a.m., Louise called Harriet Aucker, head of the ladies' committee at church. If she were going to get out of co-chairing the Harvest Fest committee with Ty Hanson, Harriet was going to have to approve it.

Miss Harriet answered on the first ring. "Hello?" It sounded like she'd been out of bed for at least four hours and had a field or two plowed and planted.

"Miss Harriet. It's Louise."

"I hope your little girl is feeling better."

"She is, thank you." Louise opened her mouth to explain the reason for her call, but Harriet didn't waste time breathing when she could talk at the same time.

"I'm glad you called. I want to run down the list of people who always do certain jobs at Harvest Fest. Then, of course, there are the places where we need volunteers. That's where you'll have to do some stomping around. I'd do it myself, but my stomping days are behind me."

Louise would have argued with that. After all, just last week, Miss Harriet had made seven hundred and fifty apple dumplings and one thousand whoopie pies and sent them along with the Bright Lights leader two hours away to the superstore where they sold every last one of them. Before she'd gone to bed for the night, she'd managed to write an article for the paper, deliver a fruit basket to a shut-in, and on the way back had pushed Lacy Dunn and her four kids out of the ditch where her minivan had gotten stuck when Lacy reached down to grab a sippy cup and ran off the road. If that wasn't stomping, Louise had no idea what was.

"Now, you come on by when you head in for your shift at the diner tonight, and I'll give you the information I have. You can get that hunk-a Ty to do the heavy lifting, but he's got more brawn than brains, so you'll have to do the thinking for both of you."

"Ty is actually really smart." Louise stood with her mouth open. She hadn't intended to say that. But in the short time she'd known him, she'd found out that was one of his sensitive issues—everyone thought he was a dumb jock. It was the label he'd gotten in high school.

It wasn't true.

"Well, you're the only one who thinks so, honey, and thinking it so doesn't make it so. But that's neither here nor there. How's that gram of yours doing? She looked pretty good in church yesterday. She feeling spry enough to make me a couple green tomato pies? I'm making a trip down south to visit some shut-ins day after tomorrow, and I'll take those with me. You can bring 'em in to the diner tomorrow. You're working every night this week to make up for not coming last week, isn't that right?"

Did she have the whole town's schedule memorized, or was it just Louise? Louise opened her mouth to say something, not sure what, as they'd been around the world and back since she'd picked up the phone, but Miss Harriet was faster than her.

"The whole town is looking forward to Harvest Fest, and it's perfect every year, so not to put pressure on you, but you want to get started right away and make sure people are doing their jobs."

"That's what I wanted to talk to you about." Louise felt like she won a major victory just getting some words inputted into the conversation.

"Huh? That's easy, honey. You just get that great big lug-of-muscle that's co-chairing with you to point those dimples at the ladies, and they'll perk right up. As for the guys, I'm sure the jock can intimidate them, but usually it's the wives who are in charge, so just focus on getting their approval, and they'll whip their husbands right up into shape, so they will."

"I don't want to be the co-chair."

"Of course you don't, honey. We don't do things because we want to, we do them because it's right. Now, make sure you stop in and get my lists. I'll be leaving tomorrow early. Thanks for the chat."

Miss Harriet hung up.

Louise stood in the kitchen holding the phone, staring at it like Miss Harriet might pick up again if she only waited long enough.

Not gonna happen. She slapped the phone down on the counter. Frustrated. She actually would love to chair the committee on Harvest Fest. She loved her town and loved serving. Loved planning things that made other people smile. But she didn't want to...couldn't...do it with Ty Hanson. She just couldn't.

Gram had already gone out to the garden, so Louise shoved those thoughts aside and grabbed her gardening gloves. She stepped out the back door and into the beautiful North Dakota morning. Mist rose from the ground, and as far as she could see, brown and green and blue stretched out until they met on the far horizon.

Gram sat over by the beans, on one of the benches Palmer had made. It was dry enough to pick them, and Gram was pulling long purple pods off the bushes and putting them into a bucket. Louise went over to the potatoes first, pulling out some weeds and reaching her fingers in to grab a few tubers to have with the beans at lunch. She had a ham bone in the fridge that would provide meat and flavor.

Mentally she calculated how many jars she had washed in the pantry. Probably enough to can a few quarts of beans, because there should be way more than they could eat today.

When Tella came running happily outside, thankfully completely recovered from her fever, Louise gave her the potatoes to take in and set on the table. "Bring me a clean bucket from the porch, too, please. And I'll help Gram pick."

Louise walked over to the bean row and bent over. She loved this variety. They tasted okay, but the deep purple bean against the dark green leaves was as pleasing to the eye as anything could be and made them fun to pick.

"Wow, you already have a ton in your bucket," she said to Gram, calculating in her head if she'd be done with the canning before having to go to work. "I'm at the diner from one to nine today."

"Ames said she'd help," Gram said easily. Gram had always been like a workhorse. Plodding along at the same pace, never rushing, just getting the work done. Louise knew she had more of a tendency to sprint then get tired.

"That will work out, then," Louise said, hoping she didn't sound discouraged. This really should be Ames's house now.

"What's wrong, dear?" Gram's hands never stopped moving, but her head turned to give Louise an assessing glance. Gram had been concerned about Pap after his stroke, but normally she didn't miss much.

Could she share her concerns about Ames needing to be mistress of her own house with her gram? Gram would encourage her to stay, of course. Although Gram was always honest. To a fault, maybe.

She checked out the house to make sure Ames wasn't lingering at the door. "I was thinking, with Ames coming here to live, maybe I need to move on."

"Because you feel like it's Ames's house now?"

"Yes." She threw a handful of beans into Gram's bucket. "In my heart, it's still yours."

"But you and Palmer do most of the work to keep things moving," Gram pointed out, her hands never slowing.

"I know. I want Ames to feel welcome and like she has a home."

"I know what you mean, dear." Gram's beans hit the bucket with a satisfying plop. "So, where would you move on to?"

Louise shrugged. "In town maybe." Gram didn't know about the money, and Louise wasn't going to mention it, although she might suspect about Paul.

"Is that the best for Tella?"

"Tella still could come out here as much as she wanted. And it would actually be easier for her to get to school. It would be a much shorter bus ride."

"True."

"Plus, there would be some kids to play with in town."

"You think Tella needs that?"

"I think so." Did she? Tella was serious and quiet for her age. There was nothing wrong with that. But eventually, Louise'd be buying her own spread.

"Sometimes kids get into more trouble with others their age. She's not lacking companionship and attention. This way, she'll work well with people who aren't her age. I'm not sure it's necessary."

Gram had said what was in Louise's heart.

"If you're thinking you need to marry Paul to get out of here, I say no. But if you're thinking you want to give Ames some space, I say that's thoughtful of you."

"Maybe Ames doesn't need space." Ames walked around the corner of the garden. "I feel awful that you think you need to leave now that I'm here."

Louise looked up for a second to smile at Ames before continuing to pick beans. "It's not that I feel like I do, it's that I think it might be better for everyone for you to get established here. This is your home. Surely you want a little privacy."

"Maybe Pap and I need to go," Gram said in the same no-nonsense tone.

"No."

"No."

Ames and Louise spoke together.

Louise gave Ames a pleading look, hoping she'd understand and not get offended. "I just want to give you the room to make this place your own home. Not mine. And not with an eight-year-old underfoot."

Ames glanced over to where Tella skipped around the garden, swinging a rope and obviously wrapped up in some kind of pretend play. "She's not a problem. Neither are you."

Louise didn't say anything. She figured both Gram and Ames would say what they were thinking, but she couldn't shake the feeling that she needed to move out of the way. At least for a little bit. And she couldn't discount the fact that if she got married, she'd have the money to buy her own ranch, with enough left over to hire help.

"I haven't made any decisions."

"You'll talk to us first?" Ames asked. "Palmer would be heartbroken if he thought you were moving out because we're here."

"I won't do anything without talking to you and Palmer," Louise agreed. She didn't say how soon she'd talk to them.

And she still hadn't solved her other, bigger problem about Ty. But maybe she just needed to man up and face him. She'd been thinking of ways to run. Maybe she just needed to lift her head and take it on the chin.

Chapter 3

Ty walked up the street to the gym. In his condo in Pittsburgh, he slept until noon and was up until after midnight. Here in North Dakota, everything shut down by eight p.m. His mother was busy making crafts for her online business. She and a friend were taking a vanload of things to a craft fair in the Cities and would be gone all week. She'd felt bad about leaving when he just arrived, but it was the way she earned her living. Renting the ranch ground brought in some but not enough, which was part of the reason she was selling.

He couldn't stand to think of her selling the ranch, but looking at it from her perspective, it made sense. She said she had someone interested, but Ty was tossing around the idea of buying it himself. The memories of his dad had faded with time, and he'd actually gotten to the point where he wouldn't mind walking in his dad's shoes.

He'd been a hockey player for so long. Could he become a cowboy again?

He assured his mom that he'd be fine while she was gone. She'd left food in the fridge, and he intended to hit up Patty's Diner for his evening meal.

As he walked down the cracked sidewalk, looking around, the town hadn't changed all that much. A few businesses gone. It looked older, weathered.

The parking spaces in front of the diner and the gym were all taken, so he'd had to park up the street. He didn't remember the diner being that busy years ago.

He reached the solid glass door of the gym and pulled it open. He hadn't expected it to be busy, either. He remembered Sweet Water as small and sleepy. Not many kids stayed after graduation. But it was a nice town to have a family in. Safe. Friendly. Everyone knew everyone else.

As he walked to the counter, which was located at the back, he nodded at a couple of people who were looking at him like they knew him. From his picture on TV, apparently, because he looked nothing like the boy he'd been when he left.

Wonder what Louise would think of him now?

He shoved that thought aside as he rented a locker and bought a one-month membership. She hated him, of course. Guys didn't do what he did and get away with it. Funny that Louise never called him out or tracked him down. The whole way through college, he half-expected her to show up. Or maybe he just wanted her to.

He shrugged that off too and made a quick call to his therapist before he started his workout with his PT on a facetime call.

Two hours later, he clicked his locker shut and slung his bag over his shoulder. It was the last year on his contract, and he wasn't going to get lax. Just because he was widely considered to be the best forward in the NHL didn't mean he would get a great offer. Sometimes his hometown seemed quaint and rural, but it had definitely taught him the value of hard work.

He chugged another drink from the water bottle he carried before pushing the door open and stepping out. His stomach rumbled. The diner had cleared out some, judging by the fact that there were several spaces available in front of it now. Eating alone had never been his thing, but maybe he could chat up the waitress. It would make a lonely meal bearable if he at least had a conversation going.

He stepped in, the little bell on the door ringing in a friendly way. He didn't remember it being this small.

The sign said "Seat Yourself," but there weren't that many choices. Two tables were empty but not cleaned. A waitress, with golden blond hair pushed through the hole in the back of her hat and falling to the middle of her back, stood with her back to him as she wrote down the order of an older couple sitting in a booth along the window.

She was slim and seemed friendly as the older couple laughed. The older lady patted the waitress's arm. Yeah, she'd do.

He nodded at a man and a boy who stared at him. Several other tables looked around at his arrival with the nosy interest of a small town. A couple of people didn't even move. Out-of-towners, probably. Or maybe, like him, they'd left and realized the rest of the world didn't stick their noses into every other citizen's business.

He took a table in the corner with his back to the wall so he could look over the room. His eyes were drawn again to the waitress as she took the order to the cook and came back to deliver drinks then clear the tables. Maybe she didn't see him come in. Or maybe she was friends with Louise, and Louise had told her what he'd done.

Doubtful. Louise wasn't a tattletale. Smart and serious, she'd made her words count. She'd probably gone and become a doctor or professor or researcher. She'd probably just come in for her brother's wedding and was long gone back wherever she lived, with her family and her life. He could stop thinking he saw her in every woman he passed.

He probably ought to be asking who the pianist at the church was. He'd forgotten to ask his mother before she left. He'd text her later when he was sure she wasn't driving anymore.

The waitress turned and carried a heavy load of dirty dishes back to the kitchen. Ty pulled out his phone. It wasn't like there were a multitude of places to eat. If this diner had rotten service, he was stuck, unless he wanted to drive forty-five minutes to the next town over, which he was going to do to see Ford and Georgia. But not tonight.

LOUISE SET THE DIRTY plates down and struggled to breathe. He was out there, and she had to wait on him. Jackson and Rebel were in the kitchen, sharing cooking duties and cleaning dirties, but she was alone out front. Normally it was tough over the dinner hour but slow the rest of the time and she could work on her editing jobs. She eyed her laptop where it sat over on the shelf in front of the big window that connected the dining area with the kitchen. Not today. She'd be lucky if she got through this without expelling her late lunch. She'd need help stringing sentences together to talk. No way she'd be able to edit a document, no matter how simple.

She had to face him. Now was as good a time as any. Setting the soda refills on her tray, she forced a smile on a face that felt like it had waxed paper pressed over it and tried to get her scattering heart to beat properly. Her shaking fingers wouldn't hold a pencil, so she decided she'd just listen to his order, using the memory tricks she'd taught herself to keep it in her head. Shouldn't be hard.

Her feet felt heavy and slow like she was heading to the electric chair as she approached his table. Wearing a t-shirt that was at least three sizes too small and jeans that hugged his lean hips, he might be good-looking to other girls. But that muscular physique had never done anything for her. It was when he started talking to her that she'd realized he was different than his clique at school would lead her to believe. Turned out he just had a silver tongue to go along with the jock's body.

A body that was much more filled out now than it had been in high school.

She took the last few steps to his table. His head was bent over the phone, but his nose was strong in profile, if slightly crooked. That was new.

Tella was a huge hockey fan, and maybe it had been subconscious, but Tella had always liked Ty's team and Ty himself. Of course, anyone who was even a casual fan of the game knew Ty Hanson.

His scent drifted up. Same undertones, bringing back those old memories, but a new and totally different overlying scent. Hard. It reminded her of heated nights and strong arms.

She shook her head. She needed to concentrate. His scent, and everything it brought to her mind, was not a part of that.

She didn't bother with her opening spiel that she might have given to a different stranger. "Menu's on your placemat. What do you want to drink?"

"Water," he said without looking up, his thumbs going a hundred miles an hour on his phone. She turned, checking on her other customers, bringing out orders that were ready, getting checks for two.

Finally, she'd kept him waiting long enough, and with a glass of ice water and a dish with two lemon slices in it, she headed back to his table. His phone was still in his hand, but he was staring so intently out the window that she actually semi-forgot her dread and looked out too, wondering what he was studying so avidly.

All she saw in the falling darkness was a slim girl, maybe in her late teens, with light blond hair, holding an armful of books and walking down the sidewalk. A boy about the same age or a little older walked beside her. The girl had her head down and reminded Louise of herself at that age, always thinking about something. Her gram said she walked around with her head in the clouds.

Ty rubbed a hand over his face and shook it like he was trying to get some thought out of his head. He braced both elbows on the table and held his head in his hands.

She set the glass down with a clank, followed by the dish of lemon wedges. "Know what you want?" she asked, as short as she could and still be polite.

He took a breath, his shoulders going up, stretching his poor t-shirt. Or lucky t-shirt, if one's mind worked that way, which hers didn't, Louise assured herself.

"Yeah." He looked up. "I'll take a..."

Their eyes met. Lights flashed, and Louise felt as though she'd been shoved, from behind, from in front, she wasn't sure, just knew that she was off-balance, off-center, and disoriented. Except for her eyes which were solidly connected to his, deep and fathomless blue. They widened. His jaw muscles flexed. His mouth went up and down, but no sound come out.

Her heart tried to dive out of her chest then bounced back, hitting the bottom of her stomach before jerking back into place, beating maniacally. Her hand rose to her chest, and her lungs sagged. But the stoic Norwegian blood that flowed through her veins helped her keep her face impassive.

"Louise," he breathed, barely audible.

She wanted to hate him. She wanted to be immune to his silver tongue and many charms. She wasn't so far out in the universe that she hadn't heard about the things he'd done and the supermodels he'd dated. She knew. And every time she heard, she told herself it didn't matter. He was history.

But her heart beat in her chest in a patchy rhythm, and feelings stirred in her chest that no one else came close to stirring. She could fall for him again. She knew she could.

"It's you." His eyes swept over her, and for a second, she was embarrassed at her jeans and t-shirt, her sloppy hairdo, no makeup, and worn, comfortable shoes. She wanted to touch her hair and fix her shirt, but then her rational mind took over. He'd been out with supermodels. She could spend all day on her hair and clothes and makeup, and she would never look like a supermodel.

Supermodels didn't have stretch marks.

The thought brought reality crashing back. She had a child, and she needed to protect her. She couldn't imagine Ty would care if he were a father. Surely the thought that a child could have been the result of what they'd done would have occurred to him if he did. But he had the money to take her child if he so desired. She needed to tread carefully.

She needed to do casual. She blinked her eyes and tried with all her heart and soul to pretend he meant nothing to her. Since he'd shown her quite plainly that she meant nothing to him. "Yep, it's me. Know what you want, yet?"

His face registered surprise. He spoke slowly. "You don't know who I am."

"Sure do. You're Ty Hanson. And I'm trying to take your order. You need more time?"

He blinked. His eyes swiped over her again. "You're—" his voice held incredulity "—a *waitress*?"

He said "waitress" the way one might have said "dumpster fire."

Louise pursed her lips as flaming pain struck her chest and fanned out. Of course, the multimillionaire hockey star looked down on her. Everyone whispered behind their hands about the girl who got herself pregnant and didn't even have a man to step up and claim her kid.

"Okay. You look over the menu some more, and I'll be back in a bit." She spun on her toes and took one step before his voice stopped her.

"Booker," he said, soft and low, but there was a note of urgency in his tone too. It hit her right between the shoulder blades, that nickname that he had made up and used when they met. It had sounded like a caress back then, sweet and deep. Like he'd really loved her like he said. Obviously, he remembered everything. Just as she did.

Her throat clenched as she tried to swallow. She tilted her head and closed her eyes for just a second. She wanted to turn around. She wanted to look into those eyes and see the truth. See that there was actually a reasonable explanation as to why he'd never come back. Hadn't even come back like a normal person did, for summer break and Christmas vacation.

But there was no reasonable explanation. As much as her heart begged her to respond to his voice, to the name shared only between them, she took a breath and walked away.

SHE WAS A WAITRESS. Louise was a waitress.

There was nothing wrong with waitresses. Nothing at all. But she'd been the valedictorian. His mother had told him that much. In a small town, anything that happened was worth talking about, and he'd latched onto anything his mother had said about anyone in the Olson family.

Louise was smart. And she'd had so many plans. She'd wanted to cure cancer, and she was a science whiz. She could have done it. She'd thought about trying premed, but she was scared she wasn't smart enough to be a doctor. He'd known she was. And he'd told her so one night while they lay on the blanket looking at the stars. He remembered leaning over her and taking her head in his hands, so much knowledge and information between his two clumsy cowboy's hands.

His words had made a sweet, dreamy look come into her clear blue eyes, and she'd told him he could do it too. He'd found out in college that she'd been right. He'd been a dumb jock, because that's what everyone thought he was. But he'd gotten a degree in agricultural science, never missed a hockey game, and never gotten any grade below an A-. Not bad for a dumb jock from the prairies of North Dakota.

He watched her walk away. Slender and small. Her head high. Her shoulders back. He'd seen her in school with that same posture, and he'd figured she was stuck-up or that she thought she was too smart to talk to the rest of the mere mortals. But after he'd gotten to know her some, he'd realized she was just quiet. After she loosened up, she was funny and sweet. Perfect.

But why was she still in Sweet Water? And why was she a waitress and not a doctor?

He tore his eyes away. People always gossiped in small towns, and he didn't want to bring attention to her. Maybe she was married. He glanced back, but her hand was under a tray now, and he couldn't see if there was a ring. She could have found a guy her senior year, although the thought bothered him, that she would forget him so easily.

But he remembered his promises to her, and he hadn't kept them. Whatever she had done, she had every right in the world to do. He'd left and broken every promise he made.

When she came back, she was just as composed as she'd always been. His friends had called her the Ice Queen in school. He hadn't thought much about it, because he'd been dating her best friend, a cheerleader. Couldn't even remember her name. He'd liked her because he thought they looked good together.

Louise came back and stopped in front of his table. Her scent, clean and pure, like a North Dakota night, drifted to him, and he inhaled like he'd been holding his breath for the last nine years.

"Have you decided yet?" she asked, with no hint of emotion on her face. She carried a tablet and a pencil this time. A lefty. He'd forgotten she was a lefty.

No ring.

Words of explanation and apology trembled on his lips, but this was not the place. He'd never told anyone about them. No one living, anyway. If she hadn't, he could respect that.

"If you need more time, I can come back."

"A burger."

Her hand moved above the notepad. Her fingers were long and slender, just like he remembered. Her hand would disappear into his.

"You want fries with that?"

"Yeah."

"Okay. I'll put it right in and be back with a refill on your water."

He hadn't even noticed he'd drained the glass dry.

They were different people now. No longer young and dumb. Just because she'd been the image in his head for so long. The girl that no other girls measured up to. The one that could laugh and be silly, while still sounding intelligent. The one he'd felt a connection with, like she fit with him perfectly. When he was with Louise, he'd felt like he was home.

Which is why it was so much worse when his dad died. He hadn't been where he was supposed to be. He'd been where he wanted to be, with all his heart and soul. He'd needed to leave after his dad's death. College was starting. But maybe the ferocity of the pull he'd felt toward Louise had kept him from returning home, just as much as the painful thought of facing his home without his dad there.

Regardless, he'd made a mistake, and he owed her an apology. He should have done it long ago, but he couldn't change the past. Today was the best he could do.

"THANKS." LOUISE TOOK the plate from Rebel as he handed it over the window.

Rebel leaned out and didn't even try to pretend he wasn't ogling Ty. "Is that Ty Hanson? The hockey forward?" He didn't wait for an answer. "I heard he was back in town. Jackson and Patty said he'd been in a few times, but I haven't seen him. Man, he's huge."

"You want to take his plate out?" Louise asked. Her tone sounded just as grumpy as she felt. Itchy. Like she wanted to leave but had to stay.

"Oh, no. I could never do that. I'd drop it on his lap." He shook his head. "I've seen him on TV. He's amazing. I can't believe he's in our diner, like *right there.*"

"He gets up in the morning and puts his pants on one leg at a time, same as you." Louise grabbed a bottle of ketchup and stuck it on her tray.

"True. But he's a *monster* on the ice. Like, seriously. I want his autograph so bad."

Louise wasn't sure she could stand around while Rebel hero-worshipped Ty. She set his plate on her tray and stalked over, not even sure why she was annoyed. Ty had lied, sure, but she didn't hate him. She'd never hated him. Okay, she might have hated him a few times when she overheard people wondering where the father of her baby was. Being pregnant in school hadn't been a walk in the park, either.

But she wouldn't be angry, and she wouldn't be bitter. She didn't want to be that person.

She stopped in front of his table, setting his plate down in front of him without meeting his eyes. She set the ketchup bottle to the side. "Do you need anything else?" she asked, proud of the levelness of her tone.

"I need to talk to you."

She wouldn't be angry, and she wouldn't be bitter.

Pasting a polite smile on her face, she said, "I'm busy. Sorry."

"What time do you get off? I'll talk to you then."

Keeping the polite smile fixed firmly in place, she said, "That's the worst idea I've heard in nine years."

He flinched, and if she were keeping score, which she wasn't, she would have notched herself a victory.

"Give me five minutes."

"I'll be busy until closing."

He looked around pointedly. Since he'd come in, four tables had cleared out, and two more were about to leave. One couple had come in. He didn't realize that she did her editing job during the slow times. She wasn't about to tell him. If he thought she was less than dirt for waitressing, he'd have to dig to find her position if he knew she had two jobs. Not counting what she did on the ranch, of course.

She squeezed her lips together, hoping that made her smile bigger, and said, "I'll be back around to check on you."

As she walked away, she remembered he'd volunteered to work with her. With all the emotion and memories, she'd totally forgotten. But he'd looked so surprised to see her. Like he didn't even know she was in town. Maybe she could fish the exact details out of Gram. Did her name get mentioned? Maybe they just said the pianist? She hadn't played when he'd been here before.

How was she going to work with him?

She snorted. Nope. She couldn't. No way.

Swiping at the table she'd just cleared, she squared her shoulders. Yes, she could. She could do anything she set her mind to. Ty Hanson was not going to intimidate her. She would be businesslike and professional, even if it was just a small-town festival. She'd tell him what to do, then she'd leave and expect him to do it. There was no need for them to spend an excessive amount of time together. And there was definitely no need for him to ever see Tella.

Then a thought hit her, so hard and fast, she actually sagged against the table. Donna, Ty's mother, watched Tella after school a lot. Every day Louise worked during the school year. What was she going to do?

Grabbing the dirties, she lugged them to the kitchen.

"You okay?" Rebel asked. "You look a little starstruck."

"Not likely." She knew Ty when he was just a down-home cowboy hoping for a break. His superstardom or whatever didn't intimidate her.

"Hey, kid, you're almost acting like you don't like him. You have some kind of grudge against him?" Jackson scratched his head. "You've never left Sweet Water, and he's not been here in nine or so years... You know him before?"

Drat! He was digging too close to the truth she needed to keep buried. She summoned a breezy look. "He went to the same school I did, but he was older by a year or several. It's been a long time, and hard to remember." She lifted a shoulder in what she hoped came across as an uncaring attitude. "He was holding me up. We've been busy, and I have a rush job I need to finish up tonight."

Jackson nodded. It was well-known in the diner that she worked on editing jobs when things were slow. Patty had okay'd it several years ago, when Louise had first asked.

She hurried around, checking out two patrons and clearing their tables. The whole time, she could feel Ty's eyes on her, burning.

Finally, when she could avoid it no longer, she walked over to his table. "Dessert?"

He stayed silent until she couldn't stand it and met his gaze at last. His chest moved in and out, like he'd been running. Maybe hers was doing the same thing. It felt that way.

She bit the inside of her cheek and looked away. "I'll give you more time—"

"Not tonight. Maybe some other time." His voice sounded almost sad, and her heart reached for him. She wanted to slap it back.

Instead, she dug in her pocket for her notepad and ripped off his check. "I can take it here, or you can pay at the register, it's up to you."

"Talk to me, Booker."

Out of the corner of her eye, she could see Rebel standing at the window. There weren't any orders to come up. She didn't look directly over to be sure, but he had to be watching Ty and her. She wasn't going to make herself a target for the town gossip. Not again.

"Stop calling me that."

"You didn't mind it when I called you that before."

"That was a lot of years ago, and I'm not that girl anymore." She lowered her voice and leaned over like she was taking his plate. "I don't know how long you're in town, but if you want an easy lay, you'd better look elsewhere." She took his plate and straightened. "I'm *really* not that girl anymore."

His jaw stuck out, and his eye twitched. "I never thought you were."

His face looked sincere, if angry. She wouldn't fall for his sweet talk again. "Fooled me." She turned and walked away.

As she carried his plate to the window, Rebel's eyes almost bugged out of his head. "You know him!"

"I told you we went to school together."

"You were talking to him, leaning over him. You guys looked real cozy."

"Yeah, Rebel. Because I hit on every cute guy that comes in here."

"Actually, you don't. Which is why this is..." His voice trailed off, and he got a puppy-dog worship look on his face.

Great. Louise figured Ty had decided to walk his check to the cash register.

"Ask him to sign my hat," Rebel said in a fast whisper.

"Ask him yourself." Louise knew she was being waspish, and she was never waspish, but she couldn't seem to stop herself.

She walked to the register. She could be kind. Just a few more minutes and he would leave. One thing was for certain, though. If he were staying in town, she'd either need to figure out how to deal with him, or she needed to take Tella and leave. Probably the second.

He stood in front of the register, and she slipped over behind it. He'd grown. Wider and taller. He always had made her feel small and feminine, but the effect was more pronounced now.

Do your job. "How was your meal?" she asked, just like she asked every stranger who came through. The locals chattered and gossiped while they paid. Ty wasn't a local. Not in her eyes.

"It was fine. Company was finer." He paused. "That wasn't a pickup line. It was the truth." He handed her cash.

"I didn't know you knew what that was." She smiled sweetly at him, staring at the cleft in his chin, which was a big mistake. Just like Tella's. She ripped her eyes away, concentrating on giving him the right amount of change.

"Thank you and have a great evening," she said before turning her back and walking blindly over to the counter where the silverware waited to be wrapped.

It took a minute before the sound of his boots on the floor signaled that he was walking out.

Relief mixed with some other emotion tore through her soul, and she suddenly felt like crying. She'd never really cried when he didn't come back. For a long time, she had a solid faith that he would. Then she had a baby and didn't have time to cry.

She looked around. There were only two tables left. "Rebel, keep an eye on those for me, please. I need to take a break."

She didn't care what he thought. She needed a minute. Walking through the kitchen, she pushed through the small pantry and out onto the protected porch. Feeling weak and tired, she sank onto the first step, holding her knees and rocking slowly back and forth. She'd barely talked to him, and she felt like she survived the firing squad. Somehow, she needed to get a hold of herself. She just had no idea how.

Chapter 4

Ty knew he was borderline stalking. But he needed to talk to Louise. He hadn't meant to insult her with the waitress comment, but in hindsight, it was easy to see he had. His words weren't coming out right. How could they? He'd been so shaken up just from seeing her. Her scent, her expression, her fingers...everything about her stirred him. Not a "normal" reaction. Not a reaction he'd had to a single one of the women he'd been around since he left Sweet Water. And yes, he'd been around, been chased, by a lot of beautiful women.

So he stood across the street, leaning against the movie theater storefront where he could see the diner. He pulled his hat down low against the stiff breeze that had sprung up, as it often did in Sweet Water, and waited.

She'd never said what time she got off, and maybe he should just let it go, but he'd let it go for far too long. He took the easy way out. Burying himself in his studies and in hockey and his friends at school. His dedication had paid off in the draft, and now in his paycheck, but he'd hurt people along the way. Not just Louise. His mother lost her husband and her son at the same time. He never stopped talking to her, but it had to be hard to only have him come home a couple of days each year, if that.

When his mother came back from her trip, he needed to apologize to her too.

Tonight, Louise was here. But the longer he stood there, the more he decided he was pushing too hard. She'd said no. He should accept that, let it go, and walk away.

He pushed his hat down farther as a gust of wind whipped down the street. Seemed like there might be a storm tonight. He didn't like the idea of Louise getting off work and driving home alone in it.

The diner had emptied out by seven thirty, and he could see Louise with a computer open in front of her, sitting on a stool behind the bar. By eight, she was up cleaning, and by eight thirty, she walked out, heading down the street toward the park where his car was sitting.

He followed with his eyes, hidden in shadow, and didn't try to follow. Maybe he'd see her again, but he wasn't going to push her tonight.

Lightning flashed across the sky, turning dark shadows into broad daylight, before darkness and the crash and boom of thunder shook the air around him.

Louise never faltered but continued walking to her car. Protective instincts he didn't even know he possessed roared up inside of him. He didn't want her to go. He wanted to follow and make sure she got home okay. He wanted to hold her and feel that she was fine.

He waited until her car started and, with lights on, she drove out of town. North. He'd be going east. Alone.

Chapter 5

"Is everything going okay?" Donna sounded bright and cheerful on his phone. Going to craft shows seemed to revitalize her.

"It's going good, Mom."

"You're getting enough to eat?"

"Yeah. I ate supper at the diner last night. Figured I'd do it again."

His mom didn't say anything for a few beats. Funny that he'd been finding his own food for years, but now that he was home, suddenly his eating, or lack of it, was her concern again.

"They have good food," she finally said, and he wondered if he'd caught her at a bad time.

"Do you have a minute?"

"Yes." Her voice sounded less perky and more cautious.

"It's nothing big, exactly. I just realized last night that me staying away from here so much was probably not the nicest and most thoughtful thing I could have done. I wanted to apologize."

"Oh." Surprise colored her voice. "It's okay. I mean, it would have been nice to see you more. A lot more. But everyone deals with death differently." It kind of sounded like she was feeling her way, and he wanted to ease her uncomfortableness.

"That's probably true. But I was selfish, because you were dealing with a death too, and I just did what was easier for me. I'm sorry."

The phone was silent for a few moments. "Thanks, son. That was a rough time, and I still miss your dad. But we made it through, and we'll just keep going forward."

"Mom. I was a spoiled brat, only thinking of myself. You can admit it."

"You're my son, and I love you."

44

"I love you, too, Mom." He almost ended the call then, but suddenly he remembered, "Who is the pianist? I'm supposed to be on this committee with her, but she hasn't contacted me."

"I'm sure she will, honey. I've got to go." And his mom hung up.

He stood outside the gym, holding a dead phone to his ear. His mother had just hung up on him. Okay, not exactly, but she'd not answered his question. She must be pretty busy. He shrugged and walked into the gym.

He hoped Louise was working at the diner tonight.

LOUISE SET PAUL'S MEAL down in front of him. He jerked his head in thanks before digging into the open-faced beef sandwich.

He'd chewed for a second or two before he pointed his fork at the seat across the table. "You want to sit down? Weren't you hungry?"

Sometimes she ate with him, but she had lost her appetite when Ty showed up at the reception a week ago and hadn't gotten it back yet.

"No, I'm good," she said. She thought of Tella mentioning that she was the only kid in her small class of thirteen kids that didn't have a father at home. She also thought of the one billion dollars that could be hers if she got married.

The supper crowd hadn't come, so she had a few minutes she could spare. She sank down, grateful to be off her feet. She'd started her shift at lunch, and she worked until closing. Normally she didn't work such long hours, but since she'd been off last week, she was making up time. At least she'd gotten her editing job finished in the afternoon lull.

Paul took another bite of his sandwich and chewed thoughtfully. "Something bothering you?"

Louise tried to shake her gloom off. It wasn't fair to Paul who was sweet as he could be and really cared about Tella.

"No. I'm just tired." She put a smile on her face. "How was work?"

"Not bad." He launched into a description of a networking problem he'd been able to solve remotely that day, and Louise tried to listen.

Finally, Paul asked, "Where's Tella?"

"Home. School starts soon. Then she'll be here some after school when she's not with Miss Donna."

He got a sweet grin on his face. "Yeah, I remember milking out those last days of summer vacation. Tell her I asked about her." He tilted his head. "Maybe we can go see a movie next week? There's a new one coming to the theater on Wednesday, I think."

"That's sweet of you." Sweet. That word described Paul to a T. "I think next Wednesday would work for me."

"Okay. It's a plan."

Paul had been the first person who had come to her mind when she'd read the letter about the money. If she needed to be married, he was single and available. He also ate at the diner every night and occasionally walked her to her car. It wasn't like she'd thought he was in love with her or anything; it was more that she thought he didn't have any better prospects. Kind of like her.

So just to test the waters, she'd asked him what he thought of a marriage arrangement. She hadn't told him about the money, just pitched it more that she wanted a house of her own and a father for Tella. Both mostly true.

He'd said he'd think about it. That was several weeks ago. Since then, he'd made more of an effort to spend time with her. Like asking her to sit while he ate. They'd gotten ice cream twice, and he'd strolled around the park with her. They'd sat together at Palmer and Ames's wedding reception. And now a movie.

She didn't care about romance or love. She'd tried a version of that and just ended up with heartbreak and tears she didn't have time to shed. She just wanted the money so she could move out of Palmer and Ames's home and into her own with Tella. She didn't want to be the spinster sister who people put up with because they had to.

"I've been thinking about your offer." He swallowed and took a drink of his diet soda.

Louise ran the tip of one finger over the napkin in front of her. "Okay." Although she'd not told him about the money, she had mentioned that she would buy acreage in the area for them to live on. If he had questions about how she was going to afford it, he hadn't asked.

He nodded as he put more beef in his mouth. "We're not in love or anything, but we'd be married for real." His hazel eyes met hers. She figured she knew what he was talking about.

"Yes, of course."

"I think I'll do it. I'll be a father to Tella. She's sweet, and a man couldn't ask for a better child. You'll be my wife."

A tiny, almost passionate look passed over his face but was gone before Louise could examine it. Back when she was young and had lots of dreams, she would never have considered doing what she had done—basically asking for a marriage of convenience so she could inherit money. And when she made her offer, she hadn't known that Palmer was going to get married, or that he even had a letter, so her money could have saved their ranch and provided for their grandparents. But even though Palmer had fixed that problem, his solution had created another one—Louise being in the way.

Then she thought of Ty and all the feelings his presence had dredged up last night, keeping her from dropping exhausted into bed and falling right asleep. She needed more defenses against him. She couldn't fall for his tricks again. Not with a daughter who depended on her. Having Paul between them was better than nothing. It would be best for Tella.

"Great." It should feel good, right? She'd just agreed to get married. "I suppose, we're engaged now?"

"Yeah," he said, with that gentle, sweet look in his eye. "I guess we are."

And several beats passed. Her finger stopped on the napkin. "I have a ring from my great-grandmother. I guess I can use that."

He nodded. "I guess I was thinking about all the changes this arrangement would make and not really about anything practical. I can buy you a ring if you want."

"I'd like to use my great-grandmother's ring, if that's okay."

He nodded, putting the last of his sandwich in his mouth.

Louise swallowed down a feeling that felt a lot like disappointment. This was exactly what she wanted. Paul was not romantic, and she knew that. They did have some interesting conversations about their work and computers and even data and statistics, which they were both interested in. Today's conversation wasn't their best, but they were compatible, and they got along. This was definitely the best decision she could make.

"I'll dig it up in the next week or so."

"We can just drive over to the courthouse and get married. What day suits you?"

It sounded like he wanted to do it this week. Louise shoved down the panic that leaped up into her chest.

"I have to organize and run Harvest Fest. Let's do it after. If we do it before, I won't have time to pack and move." Like that would take very long. She had a few things in her hope chest—a relic from her romantic dreams of childhood—and their clothes. She didn't own a stitch of furniture or kitchen utensils. She'd bought pots and pans and dish towels as the ones on the ranch had run out, but she never considered them hers. They belonged to the ranch.

"When's that?"

"The middle of September."

"That's over a month away."

"I'm sorry. If you're in a rush..." The words wouldn't come out of her mouth. She wasn't ready to get married. Sure, she'd been the one to offer, but she needed time to reconcile the event in her head. "I don't have property bought, yet, either."

"That's a good point. My apartment is only one bedroom, and I don't really want to move out to your ranch."

Louise swallowed. She could do this. "This is going to be a big change for everyone. I think it's best if we have a room for Tella before we move forward. It's not like there's a big rush." She had until Christmas to get married. The letter had said six months from the date of the letter. If she wasn't married by then, the money went to a petting zoo.

"Fine." Paul's eyes were flat, and he didn't overly look happy, but he didn't seem angry, either. "Did you hear about Design Lite and the financial issues they were having?" Paul's hand landed on hers where it rested next to the napkin on the table. It was damp and cold. She forced a pleasant look of interest on her face and silently calculated how many minutes were left on her break.

Chapter 6

Ty walked into the diner. His leg was bothering him some, and he hoped he hadn't overdone it at the gym. He'd done exactly what his therapist and trainer had told him to. He even had his therapist on a video call most of his workouts, which had garnered him some strange looks, but he didn't care. He never had a problem sticking to the protocol and pushing through. It was probably the main reason he was successful—his ability to do whatever it took.

The door hadn't closed behind him before his eyes landed on Louise. Her back was toward him, but she had the same hat on as yesterday, and the same golden blond hair fell in waves out the back of it. Her hand was on the table, and the little twerp who'd been talking to her at the wedding reception had his flimsy, white paw over it. Ty gritted his jaw, tempted to turn around and walk right back out. He had no rights where Louise was concerned, but he didn't have to torture himself.

His feet, with a mind of their own, walked to the table he'd had yesterday. He figured Louise hadn't seen him come in, although she had to have heard the bell ring. Still, several more patrons came in before she rose from where she was seated and looked around the restaurant. She froze when her eyes met his. He could see her straighten and her chin lift, which made his heart sad. That she would feel like she needed extra reserves of strength to deal with him.

Maybe the best thing he could do for her was to leave.

He looked down at his hands on the table. He'd wanted to give her a pretty apology, explain everything that had been going on, and tell her things that no one else knew. The fight with his dad and what it was about, and the guilt he felt afterward. None of it excused his behavior, but maybe it would make what he'd done to her a little less wrong. Maybe she'd be able to forgive him.

But from the look on her face and her reaction to his presence, she wasn't going to be any more willing to talk to him today than she had been yesterday.

Maybe that was part of his punishment. That he didn't get to explain.

A shadow fell across the table, and her scent drifted to his nose. He breathed in, savoring the scent he'd never forgotten and always cherished.

A glass of water appeared in front of him along with a dish of lemon wedges. "Do you want something more to drink?" Her voice was businesslike and brisk.

He stared at his hands, needing the straightening of his shoulders and the extra deep breath he took to bolster his own courage.

He looked up, prepared for the jolt that always hit him when their eyes met. "I'm sorry for what I did to you. I told you I'd be back. That there would be more to our relationship than just midnight meetings, but that turned out to be a lie. I didn't mean to lie at the time—"

"Do you know what you want, or should I come back?" she interrupted him, a bored look on her face as her eyes focused on a point just above his head.

"I want you to know I'm sorry."

"Now I know." She lifted a slender shoulder, her facial expression never changing. "I'll come back for your order." She bustled away before he could say anything more.

He hadn't ordered anything, and water was free. He got up, settling his hat on his head, ignoring the curious looks of the other patrons, and walked toward the door.

LOUISE LISTENED WITH one ear while a regular customer gave his order. Ty had put his hat on and started to get up. And she felt awful.

Sure, a bunch of years ago, he'd treated her bad. But her behavior today was inexcusable. Just because she still felt the pain, just because she looked into the eyes of his daughter every day, just because she'd struggled on her own, without his help, none of that gave her the right to treat someone else so blatantly bad.

"How's the open-faced roast beef? Don't believe I've ever had that before." Mr. Jabinginsky asked, running a work-roughened hand over his thinning hair. Ever since his wife had died about three years ago, he came in almost every evening to eat.

Paul always got the roast beef. Louise smiled sweetly. "The turkey is delicious."

"You're right. I really like that. Tastes just like Myra's. I'll take that, and if you have any of that apple pie back there, I'll take a slice for dessert."

"I'll see what Patty made today. I know there's pumpkin and shoo-fly."

"If there's no apple, I'll take shoo-fly."

"I'll see what we've got, Mr. Jabinginsky."

"Thanks, kiddo."

It always made her smile when he called her "kiddo." Like she didn't have an eight-year-old of her own.

A glance at the door and out the windows at the twilight-lit streets showed that Ty was nowhere in sight.

"Hey, Louise, I need a water!"

"I need a refill, too."

"Coming right over, guys," she said as she hurried out the door that Ty had just walked through.

"Ty!" she called. He was already heading down the street.

He swung around. His eyes widened. That face, so familiar and beloved, so much like Tella's with the eyes and chin. The broad shoulders and powerful stance. She could feel all the emotions she'd carefully swept away and buried over the years come rushing back.

He'd started toward her. "Yeah?" he said as he got closer.

Whatever she'd planned to say had gone right out of her head. He'd grown some, filled out a lot. He wasn't the boy she knew that summer, what felt like a lifetime ago. But her heart raced, like it all happened just yesterday, and her legs wanted to start walking toward him. It wouldn't be hard for her to fall right back into the same mistake.

"Louise?"

His voice was smooth and deep. Steel wrapped in velvet. It sent shivers out her back and down her arms. She straightened her spine. She wouldn't allow herself to be stupid again.

Grabbing onto the first thought in her head, she said, "We need to talk about Harvest Fest."

His face registered confusion, like what she'd said wasn't anything he'd been expecting. "Um, I know I'm helping to plan it. With the pianist. But I don't know who the pianist is."

"Me."

His mouth opened. Then one side slowly curved up in the lopsided grin that made him look way too appealing. No wonder he was a ladies' man. And she'd been his first conquest.

"I'm down with that," he said, his voice coating her insides like melted chocolate.

"I'll bring the stuff to work tomorrow. After the evening rush, you can help me if you want."

"I want." His hat was pulled low over his eyes, so it had to be her imagination that felt his gaze burning into her.

"Fine. I'll see you tomorrow."

"Yeah," he said, somehow making that one word sound like the solemnest of vows.

THE NEXT NIGHT, TY waited a little longer to go to the gym. He'd timed it perfectly, because he finished his meal just as the diner cleared out. He hated that Louise looked so tired and worn. He wanted to ease her load, carry her burden, but she'd barely been civil to him, and he felt like he was pushing his luck even being with her. If he bided his time and was patient, maybe she'd loosen up. He answered the few emails that he needed to, from his agent, his coach, and the team publicist, while he waited for her to finish up for the night.

Finally, she brought some folders and two pens over and slid into the seat across from him. She didn't sigh, but he could see the relief on her face from being able to get off her feet.

He put his phone in his pocket. As he shifted, his knee brushed hers under the table. Her eyes widened, and her knuckles turned white as she squeezed the pen she held.

Was she irritated? Or did his touch affect her? His leg pricked, and he fought to keep himself from brushing her again, this time on purpose.

"Okay," she said in a very businesslike tone. "Here is the list of things that we need to have donated. Here is the list of things that we'll need to buy." She pointed to the last folder. "And this is the list of the people who have donated in the past."

She patted the legal pad beside her. "We'll need to make a list of people who have signed up to have a booth. We need to set the cost for that, and we'll need to figure out where we want the booths to go."

"If it's anything like it used to be, people are like cows. They each have the spot they've gone to for years and years, and you'd better not try anything different."

His heart twinged a little as her lips twitched. Even though she straightened her mouth out immediately, he considered it a win.

"You are right about that, and I believe Mrs. Irvin included the map of which people get which booths here somewhere." She rooted through the folders, her fingers supple, the nails short and practical. No polish.

There was no bling on Louise. Never had been. She didn't need it. She was real, exactly what she seemed. Her authenticity attracted him now, just like it had before. Stronger, maybe. Because he knew how rare it was.

"Here we go." She put the hand-drawn map on the table between them. "Oh, yeah. This is exactly the way it's laid out every year." One slim finger pointed to a booth in the middle of the row on the right. "There's your mother's booth."

He could see "Donna Hanson" written in pencil. "Yeah, we used to help her there every year."

"I bet she makes a good bit of money there. People come from all over to Harvest Fest."

"They do. It used to be the biggest fall festival in several counties."

"Oh, it still is. That's why planning it is so much pressure."

"Hey." He waited until she lifted her gaze. "Don't feel pressure. We can do this."

Her lips flattened, like she wanted to argue. But they stayed closed. His whole heart longed to make her smile.

"If it flops this year, there's always next year." It was the wrong thing to say, and he knew it before the words had faded into the grease-scented air.

"It might not mean anything to you. But this is my town. Not only do I not want to look like an incompetent idiot, but some of my friends and neighbors depend on this festival to make ends meet. I'm sure you probably don't understand that, and I get that you don't care—"

He put his hand up. "I care. I understand. It was a stupid thing to say, and I'm sorry. I'm going to work as hard as I can to make this the best Harvest Fest yet."

Her lips pursed, but she didn't argue.

He took the list of items that needed to be donated. "You read me the list of people who usually donate, and we'll start there. I can call people tomorrow morning early, and we'll meet back here tomorrow night and see what we still need."

His taking charge seemed to ease her mind, because her face had lost a lot of that pinched look.

"That sounds good," she said in a more subdued tone. "I'm sorry I flipped out on you just now."

"It was a stupid thing for me to say. I didn't mean it. I was just trying to...make you smile."

The pen flipped end over end through her fingers. She shifted in her seat. Everything that lay between them felt heavy and thick. He wished it would go away. But he knew it was his own fault it was there to begin with.

"Louise, I'm sorry about what happened—"

The bell jingled, and a lone customer strode in, walking over to the counter and sitting on a stool.

"It's okay," she said quickly, and he knew she might mean it, but it really wasn't okay.

She slid out. "I've got to get him. I'll be back."

"That's fine." He reached over and grabbed her folder. "I'll compare these and make a list."

Chapter 7

Over the next week, they met every night in the diner after the rush. Louise had to admit, Ty was doing the majority of the work involved in calling people and organizing the donations. Haybales to line the pig chasing contest. Pedal tractors for the kids' race. A big tractor for the tractor driving contest. Pies and hot dogs for the eating contests. A hundred different things. He was taking care of it all.

Which she appreciated. They'd been working well together, with her taking care of the booths, making sure everyone had the information about when they could start setting up and where the tables would be. She'd also scheduled local talent to man the mic, giving everyone an hour starting right after the parade was over and continuing on until ten at night. Everything from stand-up comedy to families that sang in four-part harmony to local bluegrass bands.

She'd started looking forward to Ty coming in. He'd eased her mind about whether or not he was going to take it seriously. After all, he'd blown off their town, and her, so completely after he'd left, she really wasn't sure he'd care enough about anyone or anything here to put the time and effort into making their festival a success.

After where he'd been, their town and its dinky little festival must seem unsophisticated and hayseed compared to the glitz and glamour he was used to. She tried not to think about that, nor about their past. And she definitely couldn't think about the fact that she was still attracted to him. Still liked him as the hard-working, kind person he'd been.

One person remained in the diner, still eating. She put his dessert order on the shelf.

Rebel picked it up. "You mind cleaning up yourself tonight? I'd like to cut out early if I could, and Jackson's already gone. His brother was coming up from the Cities today."

"Yeah, that's fine." Louise's smile was genuine, and she tried to hide her exhaustion. They were working hard at home to get the produce put up before the first frost. They'd been lucky it was late this year.

She grabbed the plate with the pie slice on it and carried it over to the man sitting at the table.

Setting it down, she smiled. "Is there anything else I can get you?"

"No thanks."

She set the bill down. "I'll be back for this in a bit."

He jerked his head at her. She walked over to the corner table where Ty had the folders spread out.

Sinking into the seat, feeling the instant relief in her feet, she slid in. "I think we've done enough for tonight."

"Yeah. Everything is under control." Ty gave her a quick grin.

Her insides rolled. She reached for the papers and started gathering them up, trying to make her heart stop hammering. Why did his smile have to be so devastating to her?

"So, what are you doing tomorrow?"

"Canning tomatoes," she said without looking up.

"Sounds fun. I'll help. What time should I be there?"

Louise's heart fishtailed in her chest before beating rapidly. Tella was staying the night at Sawyer's since once it got cold she wouldn't be able to. Louise didn't need to worry about that angle. Although it was a reminder that she needed to tell Ty about Tella. Sometime. Somehow.

The door jingled, and Louise turned. The man with the pie had just left.

She stood. "I'm going to flip the sign. Rebel's leaving, and I'm cleaning up by myself tonight."

Ty stood too. Her head tilted as she looked up.

"I'll help," he said.

He was as good as his word, and it was barely thirty minutes later when she flipped the lights out and locked the door.

"You never told me what time to show up tomorrow," he said as they faced each other on the sidewalk.

"You know, maybe you have a little more North Dakota left in you than you think."

He snorted. "What? Because I just volunteered to can tomatoes?"

"Kinda. More because your neighbor is working and you're just showing up to help." She could almost forget that he was a hockey superstar.

"Maybe I just want to be with you." His voice came out like cream over strawberries and caused her heart to stumble then gallop.

She stared at him. He'd been so good to her over the last week or so. She'd tried so hard to concentrate on Paul and what he was saying as he ate his supper at the diner, but every evening, her whole being was attuned to the door opening and the man in front of her walking in. His legs long and muscular. His bearing confident, maybe a little cocky, even.

She loved that confidence. That proud bearing. It made Paul, as sweet and kind as he was, seem mousy and almost feminine.

"Louise..." His hand came up and touched her hair.

Her whole being wanted to close her eyes and lean into his hand.

It moved down to cup her cheek, and somehow the space between them disappeared. Her head craned up, and his eyes, dark and deep under his cowboy hat, searched her face.

Her knees felt like gelatin on a summer day, and she put a hand on his chest to steady herself. Hot and hard. Her hand pricked, and fire shot down her arm.

His other hand came up, and his thumb brushed over her cheek. His touch scrambled her brain and made her forget why being with him was such a bad idea. Why she shouldn't press closer. Why she shouldn't turn her face up to meet his lips as they descended toward hers.

The chin, that was so like Tella's...

She jerked away, turning her back and taking one step. Her breath came in fast gasps like she'd just ripped herself out of the grasp of a tornado.

"Louise, I—"

His hand touched her shoulder.

"No!" She yanked her shoulder out from under his hand. What had she almost done? The man could muddle her brain faster than a hot skillet melted a pat of butter. Tella. She had to remember Tella.

Ty had already left her once, pregnant and alone. Maybe they could share the blame for that, but if it happened again, it would be all on her. She was a single mom with a child depending on her. She couldn't afford to be that stupid again.

She turned back around, her arms crossed over her chest, her feet planted. "I appreciate your help, but I don't want you getting the idea that you can breeze back into my life and pick up where you left off nine years ago."

His mouth opened and hung there. He adjusted his hat. "I...I didn't, don't, think that. I'm sorry, I—"

She put a hand up then kicked her feet into gear and walked past him, shoving aside the easy truce from the past week as they'd worked together. She'd let down her guard, and this is what had happened. She'd almost kissed him.

"I'm sorry, Louise. I wasn't thinking that. I wasn't thinking anything." His voice held tones of frustration, and she guessed it was at himself.

It made her feel bad, and she slowed. She was overreacting out of fear and protection for her daughter. Ty was a nice guy. She didn't need to be mean. But she needed to keep him at arm's length.

A sigh pressed out of her lips. "I'm sorry. I'm more upset with myself than you."

"I'm still coming out tomorrow."

She fingered the folders in her hand. "We start at five."

Chapter 8

Ty pulled into Louise's house at 4:30 the next morning. He'd almost screwed everything up last night. He'd been that close to kissing Louise. He hadn't even apologized to her properly, and he'd almost kissed her.

Not being able to keep his hands to himself wasn't a problem he was used to having. The girls that usually hung on his arm didn't cloud out rational thought and make him want to start thinking about spending the rest of his life working beside them.

The kitchen poured light out of the windows and the open door. Palmer's truck was missing, and Ty would bet he'd taken his new wife to the big cattle auction in Fargo, which is where Ty was going to ask Louise to go before she said she was canning. He hadn't been to an auction since his dad died, and having Louise by his side would ease the sting some.

He stepped up on the porch and rapped on the screen door.

Gram looked up from where she was washing and coring tomatoes and squinted. Recognition flashed across her old face. "You don't have to knock, Ty Hanson. Come on in. What brings you out so early this morning?"

He hesitated in the act of opening the door. Hadn't Louise told Gram he was coming? He glanced around. She stood at the sink, her back to him, up to her elbows in suds. Looked like she was washing jars. Well, he'd just go with it. He opened the door and walked in, careful not to let it slam.

"I heard there was some tomato canning going on around here, and I figured I'd get in on the action."

Gram's brows raised above the rims of her glasses. "You must like her an awful lot if you're coming to court this early in the morning."

Ty grinned at Gram and winked. What would Louise do if he walked over and put his arm around her? Kissed her on the cheek? Slap his face, probably.

She looked over at him. Her eyes looked tired, like she'd slept less than he did. But she gave him a smile. He couldn't read her expression. Maybe she was surprised he showed? At least she was smiling at him.

They'd gotten into an easy, if still somewhat awkward, companion-ship type relationship over the last week at the diner. Maybe he'd ru-ined it last night. Or maybe he could get it back. That little smile was a nice first step.

Her hair was pulled back in a ponytail and fell in a wavy mass down her back.

He gave his most charming grin. "What can I do?"

A large canning pan already steamed on the stove, and a smaller pan sat on a hot burner beside it. It had been close to fifteen or twenty years since he'd helped his mother can tomatoes, but it wasn't rocket science. Just hard work.

"There's a dishpan out on the back porch." She nodded her head at a door that hung partially open behind Gram. "You can take it and fill it up with ripe tomatoes from the picnic table over by the garden."

"I'm on it." He walked across the kitchen and out the back door. The tomatoes were easy to find since the porch light was on. He picked the ripest, unsure if they were going to do them all today, and walked back in.

Louise set him to work washing while Gram cored. Soon Louise had the counter full of clean jars, and she moved some dishpans around, getting more tomatoes for Gram so she didn't have to get up and moving the washed and cored tomatoes over by the stove. They chatted with Gram about how many quarts of tomatoes she'd canned through the years and talked some about the apple harvest and whether peaches were too expensive to try to get and can.

Nice, easy conversation that reminded him of his youth and the simple life he'd left. No hockey talk, no talk of the latest celebrities, and no concern over hair or makeup or their hundred-dollar manicure. Just living life.

When Louise started scalding tomatoes and putting the hot ones in the cold water, he moved over beside her. Skinning a tomato and throwing it in her pan, he asked, "You want me to go out and get more?"

"Yes, please. We're going to do all the ripe ones we have."

That was a lot of tomatoes.

"We're making salsa with the next round," Gram said behind him. "You can come help with that too. I like having a strong back around so Louise doesn't have to lift everything. Ruined my back when I did it for years."

He gave the big pan of tomatoes on the table a look. "As long as I'm here, Louise shouldn't have to lift anything. Unless she goes all stubborn cave woman on me."

Gram laughed, and he even heard Louise snort. He bumped her shoulder with his before he left to get more tomatoes.

All in all, he made ten trips out for tomatoes. In that time, the sun had come up and a beautiful morning had dawned on the flatlands of North Dakota. He'd missed this fresh-air scent and the vast expanse of land that made him feel free and a little wild. As he carried the full pan in, he used his hip to hold the door, and just as he was swinging around to slip the pan through, his eye caught the pile of shoes by the door. Not even necessarily the pile. Just a certain pair.

They were pink. And too small to be Louise's.

He blinked. That was weird. He didn't have much experience with ladies' footwear, but he was pretty sure Louise didn't have shiny unicorns and rainbows on her shoes.

Did Louise babysit in addition to working at the diner? Was the family in that bad of financial difficulty that Louise had to work two jobs? He tucked that back in his brain to pull out later. He wasn't going to be shy about asking Louise if there were money problems on the ranch. Farming was basically nothing but money problems.

Easing the screen door shut, he hefted the pan of tomatoes and carried it in.

By nine o'clock, they had twenty-seven quarts of freshly canned tomatoes sitting on a board on the counter. Pap had come out for a while, and he and Gram had eaten some oatmeal. After eating, he and Gram had both gone in to lie down for a rest as Louise cleaned the last big pot and Ty wiped the cutting boards.

His back ached.

"Did you have breakfast?" Louise asked.

"Nope. Got up and came right over."

"Then how about I make us a couple of burritos?"

"I'll eat anything." Maybe his stomach growling had been louder than he'd thought. "I'll finish scrubbing that pan for you, then." He moved over beside her. She stiffened but didn't move away.

"No. You go sit down. It's not too hot outside yet. I'll bring our breakfast out in a few minutes."

He put his hand over hers to get her attention. "I'm not going outside to sit down while you keep working."

She stilled and looked up at him. "I just figured you were tired."

"I'm figuring you are, too."

"But I'm used to this. If we were ice-skating, I'd wear out first."

"I'm not so tired I can't work for another ten minutes."

She let go of the rag, and he took it, releasing her hand. "If that's the way you want it," she said, "you can sweep and scrub the floor after you're done with the pot."

"Oh, wow. Now she's a slave driver."

"And now he complains about everything. I want to work. I don't want to work." She turned and walked over to the table.

He squeezed the rag, because he really wanted to grab her and pull her into his arms. If her back hurt half as much as his did, he wanted to soothe it.

He shut those thoughts out of his brain. He owed her this. They'd done a lot of talking before that last night, but he should never have allowed things to get out of control the way they had. Louise had been a great friend. She'd understood him. And she was a great listener. Even watching the way she helped her grandparents, he could tell that hadn't changed.

By the time the burritos were ready, he'd finished scrubbing the pan and swept the floor. "Where's your mop?"

"We'll eat first. The food is ready, and no need to eat a cold breakfast because of a little sticky tomato on the floor."

"You don't have to talk me into it."

He carried two steaming mugs of coffee out, and she carried their plates and silverware. He held the door so she could go through and allowed her to choose where to sit. The swing.

Fine by him. He sat on the other side. Careful not to touch her. Not that he couldn't. But the awkwardness between them had given way as they'd worked together, and he'd been enjoying their easy conversation. He didn't want to scare her off again.

She gave him his plate, and he handed her a mug. Their fingers brushed, and fire flew up his arm, but he kept his face carefully neutral.

They started eating in silence. She made amazing burritos. Fast, too. Like she'd done it a lot.

"Thanks for letting me come today."

"You were a great help. I'm so glad you did."

He'd never been real good at beating around the bush, and Louise had always been fine with it. "Is the ranch in financial difficulty?"

Several expressions passed over her face as her fork stilled halfway to her mouth. Guilt? Fear?

"What made you ask that?" Louise asked. Her movements were carefully controlled, and he thought she might be hiding something. Maybe he could uncover it.

"I saw pink shoes out on the back porch. Too small to be yours."

Real fear sat in her eyes for a good two seconds. Then her mouth worked as she struggled to hide it.

"Small pink shoes?" Her breathing had become fast.

He made his voice as gentle as possible. He didn't want her to be scared to tell him about her problems. "Yeah. Too small to be yours."

"Uh..."

The hand that held her fork trembled, and she dropped it back on-to her plate. He hated that she was so upset.

Thinking to make it easier for her, he said, "So, I just thought that maybe you've taken up some childcare in addition to your shifts at the restaurant? And that made me think that the ranch might be needing money."

She let out a deep breath. "Pap had a stroke a few months ago, and the hospitalization took our savings."

"I see." He had money in the bank he didn't know what to do with. His upbringing wouldn't allow him to be a big spender. He'd always fig-ured he'd come back to the ranch and his childhood home eventually, he supposed. He didn't really have big plans other than to play the best hockey he could. That was his current job. Things had shifted over the past week for him. Maybe he was developing some long-term plans for the first time that didn't involve hockey.

He didn't want to be nosy. "If you want to tell me about it, you can."

"There's nothing much to tell." She played with the fork on her plate, while he finished up the last bite of his burrito.

"None of my business. I understand."

"Not that. The ranch is still in Gram and Pap's names, so any care they receive that we can't pay for, the ranch is collateral. But I think Palmer has it figured out, and he's going to have enough money to pull us out." Her gaze shifted between her plate and straight ahead, and she wouldn't meet his eyes.

"You want the rest of that?" he asked, indicating the last third of her burrito.

She handed her plate to him silently with a lifted brow.

He grinned. "Tell me about what you've been doing and why you aren't a doctor or a researcher."

Her eyes widened before she looked away. He'd surprised her with his subject change.

For a while, he wasn't sure she was going to answer him.

But she lifted a shoulder in a gentle shrug. "There are a few reasons, but the biggest is that I don't want to leave. I love North Dakota, and I don't want to live anywhere else."

"I definitely missed it. I didn't even realize how much until I came back." He set the empty plate down and leaned his head back. "This is a land that pulls at your heart."

"Yes. That's exactly how I feel. And I did get an English degree on-line. I work in the diner, but I also have a freelance editing job that sometimes brings in more than my waitress salary."

His head popped back up at the mention of the editing job. "So you watch kids, waitress, take care of your grandparents, work on the ranch, *and* you have an editing business?" He didn't know anyone who worked that hard. Finances must be a lot worse than he'd thought. He couldn't think of a way to ask about it in more depth, though.

"It's not that much. I'm happy and busy." She closed her eyes and leaned her head back, adjusting her shoulders like her back hurt.

He longed to rub the tension out of it, but that was moving too fast, assuming he wanted to move at all. He did. The more time he spent with her, the more he wanted to. He'd changed. She'd changed. But her changes only made him admire her more.

She wasn't ready. He needed to explain what he'd done, but not today. He didn't want to ruin the satisfied afterglow of hard work completed. Instead, he shifted, laying an arm on the backrest of the swing, making sure he didn't touch her.

She tensed, but didn't open her eyes or tell him to give her space. A win, he thought.

"So what do you do?" she asked. Her eyes stayed closed, and that made it harder for him to judge if she were asking out of politeness or because she was really interested.

"I've done a good bit of traveling during the off-season. I've taken my mom on some trips. There's a bunch of charity work in Pittsburgh that I'm involved in. And during the season, everything is hockey. Kind of nice to get paid to do what I love." The first few years were great. Over the last year or so, it had become more of a job or a business. But that was fine, and he hadn't minded. Everyone had to work. Just because his job wasn't as fun as it used to be didn't mean he was going to quit doing something that made him so much money.

His agent had been hoping to get a decent eight figures for another four years or so. After playing that long, he'd be ready to retire, no doubt. Come back to North Dakota.

"You must go to the gym a lot."

"Yeah. It's part of the job."

"So you play hockey, go to the gym, and travel, working in your charities when you have time?"

"Yeah." He supposed it sounded like a wasted life to her. What, exactly, had he accomplished, other than getting rich? Was that all he wanted?

"What do you want to do yet, that you haven't done?" he asked her, really wanting to know.

She rolled her head on the back of the swing. Her toe dragged as he pushed a little with his boots planted firmly on the floor. "I'm content here. I love being with my family, working with Gram. I love our town and my life. I'm happy."

She'd had so many plans and dreams in high school. It angered him some that she'd given up and settled. Or maybe that she'd given up and was going to settle with Paul. "Don't you want more out of life?"

A white line appeared between her lips, and she straightened. "What do you want? What are you doing here anyway?"

He didn't say anything. He couldn't hardly tell her he was out here because all he seemed to want was to be with her.

"I'm sure there are lots of career-oriented women in Pittsburgh who'd just love to hang on your arm and simper while you look straight into the camera and tell the world your hometown's just a hole-in-the-wall with three dogs and a bunch of old ladies and nothing to keep your interest."

He'd said that. Almost to the word. He thought he'd been protecting her. No one in the press would bother with his dinky hometown if they thought all the action in his life was in the city. He hadn't meant for her to hear. He definitely hadn't meant to hurt her.

Her foot tapped on the floor. A staccato beat, loud in the silence.

"But I'm happy here. Content. And it might seem crazy to you, but I don't have any desire to go anywhere, and I'm glad I never left."

"I just thought you had all these things you wanted to do when we were in school."

"Yeah. Well, I've grown up a lot since then." She jerked the door open. "Thanks for your help."

Chapter 9

Ty drove straight to his brother's, Ford's, place after he left Louise. He hadn't liked the way they'd parted. It wasn't what he planned. But he hadn't expected her to be so sensitive to his questions about why she was still in Sweet Water. He hadn't realized how the words from his interviews would sound to her. How they'd hurt her.

And the girls on his arm. She didn't realize they were just photo ops. He didn't know them, didn't have anything in common with them, and wasn't interested in changing that.

There were a lot of things she wasn't telling him, too, and he didn't blame her. She didn't know him well enough to share the financial difficulties of her family. But he could help with that, and he wanted to.

Even if she chose Paul?

Maybe that's why she was marrying Paul. Lights seemed to flash before his eyes. Of course. She was probably marrying Paul because he had money. Maybe he'd offered her money to marry him. That was pretty far out there, but she'd admitted that theirs wasn't a love match, so it wasn't too crazy of an idea.

All he'd been thinking about was Louise, and he tried to put her out of his mind for a little bit. Ford and he talked on the phone almost every week—because Ty called Ford. Ty also spoke with Georgia fairly often, who'd come down with his mother several times a year, including the holidays, to Pittsburgh.

But Ty had only been to Ford's ranch twice. Summer visits of a couple of hours. In the month that he was going to be here, visiting Ford had been high on his list of things to do. The list that had been completely derailed when he'd seen Louise at the reception.

He and his brother had been close through their childhoods and early teen years. After Ford's accident, that had all changed.

He made the right off the highway onto Ford's lane. Wagon wheels with bright flowers decorated the end of the drive. Ty didn't remember them being there before.

The drive was paved. Ty had never looked into paving anything, but he remembered asking his dad once to pave their lane, and his dad had said it was way too expensive.

First the barn came into view. Freshly painted red with white trim, it was big and majestic sitting in a perfectly manicured yard. Bright white corral fences contrasted with the brown dirt they encircled. And, hey, a white fence ran along each side of the drive. Ford's business must be doing okay. More than okay. Ford didn't really mention it during their phone conversations.

Ty continued down the paved drive. Young trees now lined both sides. It had only been four or five years since he'd been here, but the changes were astounding, and they all shouted "money." This was by far the ritziest place he'd ever seen in North Dakota, aside from places sponsored with oil money, like Sweet Water Ranch on the west side of Sweet Water.

The house sported the same expensive upgrades. Two wings flanked the original two-story structure, all sided in deep red siding, trimmed in white. It matched the barn and would draw the sun's heat in winter. Smart.

Ty was happy for Ford. Ford had been a better hockey player than Ty by a long shot. But his accident had put an end to any pro dreams he might have had.

Ty pulled as close to the house as he could and looked around for a valet. Not really, but he felt like he should not only have valet service, but he was way underdressed. He made a mental note to wear a tux the next time he visited his brother.

He stepped up to the house and wouldn't have been shocked to have the door opened by a butler. In uniform. But it was Georgia, in jeans and a t-shirt, her wildly curly hair drawn up in a topknot, from which about a third of it was escaping. Her hair was so thick and curly that a third for her was a full head for normal people. He remembered many times in their childhood when people had mused that Georgia's hair must have come from a throwback gene. It wasn't Norwegian.

"Ty!" she shouted and threw her arms around him. He caught her easily. She was light and delicate. Her body frame was not like the sturdy Norwegian frame either. If he didn't know that his mother had the highest integrity, he'd suspect that Georgia had a completely different ancestry than Ford and he who were both big-boned and tall. So were their parents.

"Hey, Runt."

"Ugh. Why was I happy to see you again?"

"If you hadn't stopped growing in second grade, I wouldn't have to call you that."

"A twelve-year-old asked her out the other day." Sawyer's deep voice echoed through the hall.

Georgia rolled her eyes.

"Hey! I didn't realize you were visiting. Was the valet busy taking your car to the back lot, and that's why I didn't see him?"

"The valet took his car around back and is washing and waxing it. If you left your keys in your ignition, he'll do the same for yours." Ford limped down the hall. His blue eye, so dark it almost looked black, was as serious as it always was. The other eye was gone, the area covered in an eyepatch. All the laughing of his childhood had vanished with his accident. The right side of his face twisted in a permanent scowl, and his left side, though not affected, always matched it, at least as far as Ty knew.

Ty's brows felt like they'd fallen off the top of his forehead. "You really do have a valet."

"I do." Ford hobbled to a stop. He held out his hand. "It's been a long time, bro. Note the changes."

He'd lived too long out of the land of his birth. A cool handshake was very Norwegian, but Ty would not be put off by the emotionless greeting. He wrapped both arms around his brother who, despite his accident, was still a shade taller than him. And still fifteen months older. And still best friends with Sawyer, Louise's brother.

He stepped back and spoke to Sawyer first. "Someone told me you had so much work to do on that ranch you needed to be three people."

"That's the truth. But some people can't be convinced to leave their castle to come down and meet with us peasants, so if I want to see him, I have to come to him."

"I see. I hope I'm not interrupting?"

"Nope. I'm happy you've finally made it back up home."

"Been busy."

Ford snorted, and Georgia outright laughed. "You're not too busy to come see your family. There were other things keeping you away."

Ty painted a bland look on his face and shrugged like they'd completely missed the mark.

"I'm not standing here forever," Ford growled. "Georgia, tell the cook to make us something to eat and have that annoying maid serve us in the sitting room."

Ty's brows furrowed at his brother's brash words. He met Georgia's eyes, but she only shrugged. This was why she was here instead of living her own life. To take care of Ford because everyone felt bad for him.

Ty wondered if maybe Ford was drowning in a little self-pity, but he didn't see him often enough to call him out on it. If Georgia put up with that treatment, then good for her.

Ford turned without saying anything else. Ty glanced at Sawyer, but he was watching Georgia walk away and missed Ty's look. Sawyer's face held an odd look. Almost longing, but Ty had to be reading that wrong since he treated Georgia like an annoying kid sister.

Ty followed Ford's slowly retreating figure, knowing he shouldn't have stayed away so long. Obviously, Ford could use a brother.

THAT NIGHT, TY DIDN'T come into the diner at his usual time.

Paul had stayed longer than he normally did, and Louise had a harder time than she normally did focusing on what he was saying.

She hadn't been very nice to Ty after he'd been so kind and helped them with the tomatoes. She'd been hurt to see him with other women, and it had been even worse when he'd said there was no one worth looking at in his hometown, but that had been years ago. She was over it. If she wasn't, she needed to be.

Her upbringing demanded an apology. But he'd not shown up.

The planning for Harvest Fest was coming along well, so she wasn't worried about that, but she'd come to expect him in the evenings.

She choked on a laugh as she stacked dirty plates and cleared off the last table. She'd come to *look forward* to seeing him.

Had he not come because of how snippy she'd been? Guilt pricked her throat, and the need to apologize made her fingers twitchy.

Miss Donna was out of town at a craft show, so if he were home, he'd probably be alone. Being alone with Ty was a disaster waiting to happen. There's no way she was going out to see him. But she could call him. Except they'd never exchanged numbers.

Closing time finally came, and she rushed through the night cleaning and chores. Saying "good night" to Jackson and Rebel, she hurried down the deserted sidewalk. The town shut down at nine.

Standing at her car door, she scrolled through her phone contacts, finally finding Georgia, Ty's sister. They weren't besties, but she definitely considered Georgia a friend. She hoped it wasn't too late to call as she hit the button and waited for her to answer.

"Hello?"

"Georgia, it's Louise Olson."

"Hey, Louise. Everything okay?"

"Yes. Nothing's wrong. I just needed to talk to your brother, and I wondered if you would give me his number?" She hoped her voice sounded confident and friendly, rather than desperate.

"I can do one better. Ford's sitting right beside me. I'll hand my phone over."

"Wait!" Louise took a breath. "Not Ford. Ty."

Silence fell on the other end of the line. "Okay, let me get it."

Louise waited. Maybe, since Ty was such a big hockey star, Georgia got calls from other people asking for his number?

"Here it is." Georgia lowered her voice. "You know it's kind of a secret, and I'm not supposed to give it out to anyone, especially women."

"I'm sorry. I'm not trying to hit on Ty." She didn't want to have to explain her driving need to apologize, so she said the next best thing. "We're co-chairs of the Harvest Fest committee, and I need to speak with him."

"Oh. Okay. Of course." She gave his number, and Louise programmed it into her phone.

"Thank you."

"Maybe we'll be in—" She stopped abruptly. "Maybe I'll be in to eat sometime, and we'll catch up."

"I'd love that."

They hung up, and Louise pulled up Ty's number before she could lose her courage. She faced the warm evening breeze and relished the feel of it pushing her ponytail and fanning her flyaway hairs around her face. She pulled the clip out of her hair, throwing it in her car and running her fingers over her scalp, lifting the flat strands and allowing the breeze to ease her tiredness.

It seemed to take a long time before he answered. "This is a private number. What do you want?"

She blinked at the abrupt tone and voice on the other end. "Ty?"

"Don't call again." He hung up.

How had he known it was her? Louise stood beside her car, uncertain. Wow. He was a lot angrier than she'd thought he should be. Of course, she'd been rude, but she'd not been that bad. Had she?

Or maybe he'd thought she was one of the random people who called because he was a sports star?

She tried again.

"I told you not—"

"It's Louise."

His voice cut off immediately. "Louise?" he asked in a much softer, gentler tone.

"Yes. Are you at home?"

"I'm on a four-wheeler halfway between our place and town."

"I'd like to talk to you."

"I can be at your house in twenty minutes."

"No." She snapped out, not meaning to be mean, but he couldn't be at her house. Not while Tella was there. "I'm sorry, but my grandparents go to bed early."

There was silence on the phone. Then he said slowly, "You could come to my place." A short pause. "My mother is at a craft show."

"I know." She didn't want to say that it wasn't a good idea. She might as well say she knew she had no self-control where he was concerned. Where could they meet? She hadn't thought this through. "Could we meet at the church?"

"Uh, sure. I'll just keep coming in. Be there in ten."

"Ty?"

"Yeah?"

"Thanks."

Chapter 10

What could she want?

Ty parked his ATV at the end of town and walked up to the church, maybe a little amused with himself that all Louise had to do was ask and he did whatever she wanted. She could have asked to meet him in Texas, and he would be heading toward the nearest plane right now.

Why? He'd barely even talked to her for the last nine years. He didn't even really know her. Why did he react to her like she was the only girl in the universe?

And after she'd been so standoffish since he'd come back. He deserved it, of course, but thought he'd been making headway. Then she'd closed off again earlier today. He'd thought maybe he just ought to let her go. She didn't want him, and he needed to accept it. It hadn't made him mad, only sad and guilty.

He walked to the church, but she wasn't sitting on the front steps. In his childhood, the church had never been locked. But he'd been gone a long time. A lot of things had changed in the past nine years.

Walking up the steps, he tried the heavy wooden door. It opened easily. He stepped inside the dark interior, giving his eyes a few minutes to adjust. They were used to the dim light outside, so it didn't take long.

"I'm sitting in the back pew on this side." Her voice came out of the darkness. He could make out her light t-shirt and walked carefully over.

"I'm wearing dark blue. You probably can't see me."

"I can see your outline against the stained-glass window."

He turned his head, and sure enough, he stood directly between her and the window. "Want me to stay here?" he asked softly, not wanting to push her or scare her away.

"Wherever you're comfortable."

He'd be comfortable close beside her, their legs touching, and his arm around her. Something told him she wouldn't.

He shoved his hands in his pockets. There was about five feet between them, and as his eyes adjusted, he could make out her face. Probably if he moved from the window, she could make out his. He chose her pew but sat on the end, leaving plenty of space from where she was in the middle.

"We seem to do better in the dark," he said.

"Better?"

"At least we're talking to each other."

"I thought with meeting in the church, talking was all we'd do." She seemed to allude to the fact that they were attracted to each other. It shouldn't make him happy, but he was glad she felt it too.

"I won't touch you." He'd tried hard not to make promises he couldn't keep. That one would be hard. Already he wanted to touch her hair, run his hand over her cheek. He put his elbows on his knees and rested his forehead on the pew in front of him.

She shifted, and the scent of her drifted to him, mixing with the lemon polish and soulful church scent. The setting didn't keep him from wanting to be closer.

"I'm sorry for being rude today. I...I don't usually act like that, and I'm embarrassed at my behavior. Please forgive me. I'll try to do better."

"I don't blame you for the way you acted."

"It was still wrong. I'm sorry."

"I deserve that and a lot worse."

She was quiet. Maybe that meant she agreed. He wasn't sure.

"How'd you get my number?"

"Georgia."

"Ah." His small town. Of course.

"I can delete it if you don't want me to have it."

"No. I'm glad you have it. Call me anytime. I have your name programmed in now."

"Does that mean you will or you won't answer with a bark and a growl?"

He laughed, lifting his head. "Sorry about that. I get calls..." He didn't finish. She didn't need to know about the crazy women whose calls he got.

The church seemed to breathe around them. A quiet, peaceful place. Filled with memories of worship and song. "This was a good place to meet."

"I love it here."

She'd said that about the river where they met too.

After a while, he asked, "Did you have something else you wanted to say?"

"No. I just wanted to apologize." She breathed out. "When you first came back, I cut you off when you tried to, and I'm sorry. If you have anything else to say, I'm listening."

"I do. But I don't want you to run off."

"I won't."

She'd keep her word. She always had. He could trust her with everything.

He steepled his hands together and allowed his head to hang down. The darkness gave a bit of privacy, and he felt more free to let his emotions course through him.

She was giving him the chance to apologize. He was going to explain, too. He wanted to do it right. Because he'd never stopped thinking about her.

"That last summer, all those years ago, I'm sorry for leaving you the way I did. Something happened before we met for the last time, and I didn't tell you about it when we met that last night." To be honest, they hadn't done much talking that night. The other nights, they'd spent hours talking and maybe kissing some. But that last night, there had been a desperation because of his impending departure that had pre-cluded any talking. He wished he could take it back because Louise de-served better.

She didn't say anything, didn't move, and if she were breathing, she did it so quietly he couldn't even hear.

"I fought with my dad."

One beat while she processed what that meant, then she gasped.

"Yeah. The last words I said to him were not nice." He let his breath out slowly, not wanting to go back to that time. There were so many other memories that were precious to his heart, but he wished he could erase that argument with his dad. "He and I were talking."

His throat closed, and he stopped speaking to wait for it to relax.

"You two were close," Louise whispered.

So true. Even as a teen, wherever his dad went, he went too. His dad coached his hockey teams, and he worked on his dad's farm, doing anything that needed to be done. He loved his dad and loved spending time with him. He knew his dad was proud of him, and after Ford's accident, he and his dad got even closer, like his dad had realized the fragility of life.

"We never fought. And I never did anything I wasn't allowed to do. I mean, of course I was a kid and did stupid stuff, but..." He lifted his head and turned it, laying it on the back of the next pew, looking at Louise's gray features. "Peggy sent me that note." He finally remem-bered her name. His girlfriend Peggy had been best friends with Louise. Ty suspected now it was so Louise could help her with homework and studying, but whatever. "I told Dad where I was going that night. He knew I was meeting Peggy. He knew I didn't really care about her. And he trusted me so much he wasn't even up when I came home."

He hadn't been heartbroken about Peggy, but he'd been intrigued with Louise. So intrigued, he'd asked her to meet him again, and she'd agreed.

"Anyway, he didn't know about me sneaking out to meet you, but I felt guilty about it. That last night, while we were doing the evening feeding, I finally came clean. I admitted what I'd been doing—meeting you—and that it had been totally innocent, but I told him..." He wasn't sure he should admit this. He'd never told Louise how, exactly, he felt. But he let it out. "I told him I loved you and was thinking about staying on the farm so I could be with you. Just a year until you graduated."

Louise shifted and moved, like she was uncomfortable, but she didn't say anything.

"He was adamant that I not forgo college. And the more he insisted, the more I felt like he was trying to come between us and to keep me from the most important thing in the world, which used to be him but was now...you."

Chapter 11

Louise could hardly breathe. Her lungs froze then spasmed. Her heart beat erratically, and her hands felt clammy as she gripped them together in her lap.

She kept her mouth tightly pressed shut.

"I didn't even bother sneaking out that night. I was headed to college, full ride on hockey, and he couldn't stop me."

"I knew you were upset," she said, her voice barely audible. "I thought it was because you were leaving."

"Partly. But yeah, that fight with my dad, all the emotions. I knew he was right, and I knew I'd do what he wanted me to, but I hated that I had to leave the person I wanted most in the world. I was selfish that night. I took what I wanted. I never intended to hurt you. I was going to keep all my promises, I swear. But Dad was already gone by the time I got home, and I never talked to him again."

Silence lay between them. Her heart broke for him. She'd never known he'd fought with his dad and hadn't had a chance to reconcile before he died. As close as they were, that had to have eaten at him all these years. Ty would have been devastated, not only by his father's death but by the fact that they could never make up.

There was one thing that bothered her. Louise knew this wasn't the most important takeaway from everything Ty had said, but as a mother, it was the one that drummed in her heart. "Did your dad talk to your mom about what you and he had fought about?"

His shoulder lifted in a shrug. "Probably. I don't know. They talked about everything. So, if there was time, he probably did. I never asked my mom exactly how things went that night. I don't think I want to know."

Miss Donna might have been like a grandmother to Tella because she knew she *was* Tella's grandmother.

Louise sat in the still, sweet silence of the church, knowing she should tell Ty about his daughter but unable to summon the words. After hearing everything he'd said, she had a much better understanding as to why he'd left.

"So, you've probably figured out by now that once Dad died, my guilt for our fight, and the thought that it caused his heart attack, and all that, is why I never tried to contact you. It was like I couldn't make up to him what I'd done that night, the fight, the disrespect, the break in our relationship, but I could give up what caused it to try to atone."

"And that was me."

"I'm sorry."

Maybe she should stay angry. Maybe she shouldn't feel his pain so acutely, but she wanted to reach over and comfort him. Put her arms around him and share his burden.

She spoke the words in her heart. "I don't think your dad would feel that you needed to atone."

"I know. He wouldn't."

"And maybe some of that was that he never got to see you play."

"Yeah. I've thought of that too. Every single time I do something on the ice worth celebrating, I want to look in the stands and see him there. It hurt too bad to come home." He straightened and twisted in the bench so that his torso faced her. "After a while, not reaching out to you was like a penance."

He leaned forward, and she thought for a moment he was going to break his promise not to touch her. But his hands fisted, and he dropped them on the bench between them. "I wanted you more than anything. Through college, through the draft, through the NHL and all the stuff I had to do, but after a while, it felt like it was too late. After a month, it would have been hard. After a year, almost impossible. I felt like there was no chance for us."

"Oh, okay. I guess that's when the supermodels came in." She hated the flippant tone of her voice, but Palmer and her pap watched a lot of hockey. She couldn't help but see him. Tella loved him. He was her favorite player, because Palmer had said he came from their hometown. Louise couldn't say that the connection went even closer.

He ignored her statement. "It seemed like there was no chance. But when I came back and saw you at Palmer's wedding, everything I'd ever felt for you, and never felt for anyone else, ever, hit me hard." He spread his hands out between them. Large, strong hands.

Louise couldn't stop looking at them.

"I know I don't deserve it, but I'd like a second chance."

Every beat of her heart shouted in the silence, "Yes, yes."

"I just told Paul last week that I'd marry him."

She didn't want him to tell her to go back on her word. She didn't want him to take her word that lightly.

He didn't say anything for a bit, and relief cooled her chest.

"Is that what you want? Is that what you really want?" he whispered instead.

The answer was easy. "No. But I haven't made a single decision to do what I wanted, *only* what I wanted, since you left." He would never understand why. Not until she told him about Tella.

"Tell me that you don't feel anything for me, and I'll leave you alone."

"I—" Oh, but it would be a lie. "No lying."

"No lying," he repeated.

"I trusted you once before."

"I know. And I failed in a big way. I'm sorry. I wish there was something I could do to show you how much."

There wasn't. The only thing would be time. Unless she made herself trust him.

When she didn't say anything, he said, "Could we, maybe, be friends? And you just know that I want more. And put Paul on hold?"

She threw her hands up. "I don't even know how that would look! You've got a whole life far away from here. A whole world that I don't know anything about! I don't know anything about you as a person."

"Hey. Hey. Shh." He didn't touch her, but he slid closer. "How about we just take it a little at a time?"

And this was where she should tell him about Tella. There was no reason not to tell him, except...she was a coward. For so long, it had been her secret. Only hers. But there were other things, things that had run through the back of her mind since he'd come back.

How would that work out? Would he take Tella? Maybe he'd want Tella to live with him. And Tella was such a big fan, she might. Louise couldn't hide her forever, and he was going to find out, but it was too much for tonight.

He stood beside her, bigger and stronger than she remembered. The attraction was still there.

"I need to get home. My family will wonder where I am." Distance. She needed distance.

"Yeah." He followed her out the pew. "Booker?"

She smiled at the nickname. "Yes?"

"I know I don't deserve it, but please, give me as much of a chance as you've given Paul."

"Maybe I have some secrets that I need to share, too, but not tonight."

"Tomorrow?"

"No." That was too soon. "Give me a couple of days."

"You're working at the diner this week?"

"Not tomorrow. Friday." Sawyer was coming in then to take Tella to his ranch one last time before school started, which worked out nicely since Palmer and Ames were going south to a cattle auction. They were feeding the stock before they left. "My shift starts at three. Maybe we could meet at two?"

COWBOYS DON'T HAVE A SECRET BABY

"I'll try to be out of bed by then." His teeth flashed, and she remembered his self-deprecating sense of humor.

"You'll probably be up at dawn jogging or something."

"No, not yet. No one knows this. But the reason I came home in the first place is because I tore a few ligaments, not doing hockey, and I needed surgery to repair them. My agent doesn't want anyone to know, because it could hurt my monetary prospects as he negotiates a contract." He opened the heavy door for her, and she walked out.

"I see. So you're expecting to completely recover."

"Yeah, not a big deal. Just takes some time. It's nice that Sweet Water has a gym in town now. Makes it easier. I don't have a long drive every day."

They stopped at the bottom of the steps. Her car was back toward the diner. He'd probably parked on the other side of town.

"Booker?"

She looked up at him, not touching. He'd promised, and he'd kept the promise.

"Yes?"

"Thanks." He ran a hand through his hair, free from his hat, and hooked it around his neck. "I know this wasn't easy for you."

"No. It wasn't. But I'm not perfect, and I've made some mistakes, and I hope that people will forgive me, too." She didn't know if he'd be angry about Tella or not. She didn't feel like he had the right to be. If he'd have called her, even once, she would have told him she was pregnant. It would have been a relief. But maybe not. Part of the reason she hadn't sought him out was so that he could play the hockey he was born to play. If he'd come home to do the "right" thing and marry her, he wouldn't be where he was. It was a sacrifice she'd made on purpose.

His hand dropped. "I'll see you Friday."

"Yeah."

"At two."

"Yeah."

"I only said I wouldn't touch you tonight."

"We've got a cattle prod at home. I'll change the batteries and bring it."

He laughed and held his hands up. "Ford used one on me once. I dropped like a rock. He got in big trouble."

Louise laughed. "I'm sure Sawyer and Palmer did the same thing at one time or another."

He took a breath in through his nose. "I'd like to make sure you get home okay."

"I've been driving myself home since I was seventeen."

"I know." He shoved his hands into his pockets. "Don't think I'm a stalker, but I watched you walk out of the diner a few nights ago, and with the lightning and thunder, it was all I could do not to follow you."

He'd watched her? Maybe she should be aghast at that, but the fact made her happy. "I'd think you're a stalker, but only a recent one, since I haven't seen you for almost a decade."

"You gonna rub that in for the rest of my life?"

She shrugged and tossed her head, starting away.

"I'm gonna follow you. I'll take the fields home."

The way she'd gone when they'd met at the river. He stood waiting for her answer, and she was certain if she said no, he'd respect her choice. "That's fine."

"I'll walk you to your car."

"I can make it that far, I promise."

"Humor me."

She shrugged and started walking. She couldn't deny that it felt good for someone to care.

They walked down the sidewalk in silence, Ty's big body close beside her. She could feel the heat coming off in waves. Everything that was completely missing when she was with Paul surrounded her in 3D with Ty.

She hadn't wanted to marry Paul, but if she didn't, she could lose her chance to have a father for her little girl and get the one billion dollars. It wasn't an opportunity that came around often. Or ever. And Paul was a sure thing. Ty had already left her hanging once.

It wasn't entirely fair to hold that against him, but what if something else happened? Would he leave and never come back? Paul had grown up here, gone to college, and come right back, living in an apartment as a bachelor for the two decades since. So he was almost forty. That didn't matter. An age difference of ten years wasn't a big deal. Paul loved Tella and was excellent with her. That was what really mattered.

"What are you thinking about?" Ty's voice came easily beside her.

"Paul."

He grunted. "It's not looking good for me if I've got you right beside me and you're thinking about him." He hissed out a breath. "Booker, tell me you don't have feelings for him."

"Feelings didn't get me anywhere the last time."

He huffed and looked away. "I have to live that down. I need some time. I can't erase something like that overnight."

At least he knew it and didn't expect her to fall into his arms as soon as he said "sorry." "Paul and I already have plans."

"How soon?" he asked. There was a thread of desperation in his voice, but she had to believe it was because he was used to getting what he wanted. She'd seen pictures of him with beautiful women on his arm. He had a reasonable excuse for not contacting her, but it wasn't like he sat alone in his apartment dreaming about her every second.

"After Harvest Fest."

They'd reached her car, and she clicked to unlock the doors. He put his hand on her latch but didn't open it.

"I just have a few weeks."

She lifted a shoulder. She was too attracted to him. She wanted him too much. He'd hurt her too badly once. Did she even want to go down that road again? Not likely. As soon as he left and she didn't have to see him, it would make things easier.

She shook her head. "Ty, I like you. I don't know if you're the same guy you were when we were younger—"

"I can show you who I am," he interrupted with soft vehemence. "Please let me."

"You don't know me, either. There might not be anything but some wicked attraction between us."

He put his hand up in a "stop" signal. "Don't discount that. I've been with a lot of women, and you're the only one that makes my insides feel like scrambled eggs."

She hated that he'd been with a lot of women. "Doesn't sound like a compliment."

"It was."

"That was a good point, though. You've got all these other women. Maybe you're just chasing me because I didn't fall into your arms as soon as you smiled at me."

He shrugged. "Maybe that's part of it. Maybe it's hard to find a girl who doesn't go all cow-eyed because I'm a good hockey player." He said that without arrogancy. Just stating a fact.

"You've found plenty of girls, I'll give you that."

He leaned down so their eyes were more level. His voice was gentle but firm. "Maybe the reason there were a lot is because I couldn't find the one that was better than you."

"And maybe you like variety. Or maybe you don't know how to stay." She met his eyes. He wasn't going to intimidate her. And she wasn't going to not tell him what was in her heart.

"Maybe, if I find the right girl, I'll quit hockey and take up ranching again."

"You'd better tell your mother, because she's talking about selling the ranch."

"I know. I'm thinking about buying it. I should have done it before this."

Louise wasn't sure what to make of that. She didn't think it would happen. Ty was too big of a star to quit and lower himself to ranching again. Plus, she'd already talked to Miss Donna about buying.

"You gonna open my car door?" Louise asked, pushing her other thoughts aside.

But he didn't move. "What are you doing Friday after work? I'll take you out."

Her heart jumped, and her shoulders buzzed. But... "I'm going to a movie with Paul." They'd had to reschedule after something urgent came up with his IT work.

Ty's lips flattened, but he just nodded. "What about the next night?"

"Paul and I are getting married for reasons other than our 'feelings,' but it hardly seems right to go out with another man."

"So tell him you're checking out the competition. Or tell him we're friends. I can tell him he's going to have to work for you if he wants you." Ty stared down into her eyes, as though promising he'd work for her.

Louise pressed her lips together and looked away.

Ty leaned over again. "If he wanted you, why wasn't he waiting for you when you got off work? Or better yet, he could have been working with you. Why aren't you rushing to his apartment when you're done, and why aren't you slapping my face and telling me to get lost?"

That was a good question. If she wasn't interested in Ty, she should send him on his way. And if she were going to take a chance on Ty, she should break it off with Paul immediately. It wasn't right to waffle between the two.

She knew which one she wanted; she just didn't know if she could trust him. And Paul, even if he was boring, was a sure thing. A sure father and a billion dollar sure thing.

"Paul's willing to marry me. I'd have a home here, with my family, and he'd never leave me." She met his eyes, unfathomable in the dusky light, before lifting her chin and getting in her car.

He put a hand on the door so she couldn't shut it. "I can do those three things too."

"Paul *wants* to. And you already had the opportunity." She gave his hand a pointed look. He moved it slowly, his eyes never leaving her.

"Thanks for meeting me," she said before she closed the door.

Chapter 12

Ty wasn't supposed to be jogging on his leg, but he did it anyway, wanting to get to his ATV quickly. He could go road speeds on it, but he hadn't worn a helmet. Bugs would be a problem, since there was no windshield. Not that he hadn't done it plenty of times in the past, but somehow, when he was eighteen, he didn't think about losing an eye.

His leg twinged a bit, but it held up with no searing pain as he got to his machine and started it. He hadn't wanted to take it through town, which was why he'd parked where he did. It was loud and not street-legal anyway. It used to be, but they'd not kept up with the changing regulations, he was sure. He ran down the opposite road out of town and took a left on Mr. Thompson's field road. The ATV headlight wasn't the brightest, so he had to take it easy.

It had cooled down since the sun set, and with the wind hitting him, it could even be called chilly, but it was nothing compared to the cold that winter brought, so he did what he'd done every year he'd lived here, sucked it up and told himself he wasn't that cold.

He was eager to catch up, so he didn't dawdle, but he'd always loved night in North Dakota. Everything was bigger. The sky was bigger, there were more stars, the starlight was brighter, the whole atmosphere seemed to be filled with night air and sounds. Nowhere else on earth could compare to a late summer night in North Dakota. He'd forgotten.

Feelings stirred in his chest, and the land called to him, pulling him, making him wish he'd not stayed away so long and that he was actually home to stay.

He loved hockey. He'd worked hard to be an elite athlete, but he loved North Dakota more. Maybe he'd needed to move away to know that. But there was a woman here who made him think that maybe he'd played enough hockey.

Those thoughts surprised him. Nothing came before hockey.

He hit the end of the field and slowed to make the turn on the road. She'd passed by here already, he was sure. He couldn't see lights in either direction. But he turned right and gunned the motor, riding in the middle of the right lane.

She must have been driving slow, waiting on him, because he caught up to her in the next five miles. After that, they traveled together at about 45 mph. He'd rather be in the car going home together.

The thought gave him pause. All the time he'd spent dreaming about her and wishing for her, he'd never really thought of family and home. But nowhere he'd been in the years he'd been gone had been conducive to thinking about having a home and family. College certainly wasn't. Hockey wasn't. And he'd never want to try to raise a family in the city.

Was Louise thinking of having children with Paul?

The thought made a jealous monster rumble in his chest. He'd never really wanted children, but with Louise, she could change his mind.

He backed off as she pulled into her driveway. It was long, and the house wasn't visible from the road. He followed at a distance, knowing he'd take the field road that turned off a hundred yards from the house and would follow it out to where it passed the river where they'd met.

Stopping at his turnoff, he waited for her to get out. The porch light was on, and she turned and lifted a hand before walking up the steps and disappearing into the house.

LOUISE SHUT THE PORCH light off and leaned against the door. Her heart wanted so badly to be with Ty, but her mind told her Paul was the safe choice.

"Did I hear a four-wheeler?" The only light in the kitchen came from the light over the sink. Gram stood in the living room doorway, probably on her way to the restroom.

"It was Ty Hanson."

Gram stopped her slow progress. "Oh." A little smile played around her mouth. "I see."

"We're planning Harvest Fest together, remember?" Not that they'd talked that much about it.

"I remember." Gram kept smiling as she hobbled to the restroom. Louise puttered in the kitchen until Gram made it back to bed. Then she climbed the stairs, checking on Tella, who slept soundly, before creeping to her own room.

Her phone buzzed. She pulled it out of her pocket. A text from Ty. Throwing herself across her bed with a happy little grin, she pulled the text up.

Thanks for talking to me tonight.

She couldn't wipe the silly smile from her face. Maybe this was what it felt like to be courted. Spending the evening talking to someone and still wanting to talk, even after they'd parted. Ty and she had never lacked things to talk about.

Thanks for meeting me, she texted back.

You're even more beautiful now than you were in high school.

I wasn't beautiful then. Or now.

You're beautiful because you're real. And honest.

Guilt squeezed her chest. She hadn't been either with him. If she had, he would know right now that he was a father. That they had a daughter together.

I'll see you around.

I'm going to see you in just a few minutes when I close my eyes and fall asleep. Good night, Booker.

She rolled her eyes, but her silly smile was back and stuck on. **Good night.**

FRIDAY MORNING, LOUISE sat on the bench outside Patty's Diner. Her leg bounced up and down. She'd already stopped it three times and tried to act normal, but she couldn't quell the dinosaurs that rioted in her stomach.

Palmer and Ames hadn't bought a bull at the auction the other day, but they'd gotten a lead and gone out today with the trailer, taking Tella along with them.

Palmer had texted that he'd bought a bull and would be home early. He was dropping Tella off on his way through. Which was fine. It actually worked out better in some ways, because the neighbor lady that often helped them watch Gram and Pap had not wanted to be late that evening. So, Louise had been able to tell her that Palmer would be home well before supper. The problem was, as much as she loved seeing her daughter, Tella would be here when Ty arrived, and she'd not managed to get the words out of her mouth the last time she saw him informing him that he was a father.

Sitting in the church pew with all the privacy in the world would have been a much better time to tell him than while Tella was standing over them, watching. She didn't want to hurt her daughter by springing the identity of her father on her like that. It might be different if Ty weren't a big sports star, but Tella could even be wearing his jersey today. In fact, Louise thought back to three this morning. Yep. Tella had Ty's jersey on.

Thankfully, just then, Palmer's truck rumbled down Main Street with the silver stock trailer rolling behind. Louise jumped up, meeting them before they even pulled to a stop. She opened the back passenger door.

"Tella! Honey, I missed you!" She grabbed Tella in a hug that surprised her sweet daughter. Tella hugged her back.

"I missed you too, Mom, but we had a great time! There were so many animals at that ranch, and Uncle Palmer said I could get a Brown Swiss if you said yes, and we ate junk food and fast food all day, and I even had a soda, but now I have to pee. Let me out, please."

Louise blinked. Her daughter was normally calm and quiet. She stepped back so Tella could run into the diner where she was just as at home as her own home. Louise saw the Hanson name and Ty's number, twenty-six, as Tella ran away. "Tella, wait!" But it was too late. Tella had disappeared into the diner. As soon as she came back out, Louise was going to send her back in to change. She grabbed Tella's backpack with all her extra clothes and blankets. She had no idea how Ty was going to react to any of this; she didn't need to complicate the situation by having him find out that his daughter was a huge fan.

"I think she had a really good time. I've not seen her that wound up in ages." Palmer looked back at Louise. "Are you in some kind of rush?"

"No. Uh uh." Louise slammed the back door shut and stood at Ames's window, which Ames had wound down. "I just didn't want to hold you guys up. I know you have a bunch of work to do to make that bull feel at home." She hoped it wasn't obvious that she wanted them to leave, *now*.

"We have a few minutes to talk to you." Palmer shoved the truck in park and opened his door.

Panic crawled up her throat, although she wasn't even sure why. Ty was going to find out; she needed to accept that. But maybe she didn't want an audience. No one, and she meant no one, knew who Tella's father was. "You don't have to."

She wasn't ready. Maybe she'd never be ready. But she didn't want to have to face everyone's reactions at once. She couldn't handle it if they all ganged up on her. And what about Tella? She didn't need to see everyone's reactions, either. It probably wasn't going to be pretty, and Louise wanted to protect her daughter more than anything.

But Palmer was already walking around the front of his truck, carrying a small bag. "I bought you this." He held up the bag before reaching into it. Louise tried not to tap her foot impatiently or, worse, grab the bag. Why wouldn't he just leave? She needed to figure out how to hide Tella, and he was wasting her time.

He pulled a dark blue t-shirt out of the bag. It said, *I'm a single mom. I can do anything.*

Palmer grinned.

Ames said, "How could we not think of you when we saw this?"

"I love it. It's amazing." Louise tried to tamp down her impatience, but it came out in her words.

Then her heart lurched to a stop and her brain told her to turn and run, because Ty's expensive rental car pulled to a stop in front of Palmer's truck. Sawyer's old beat-up pickup stopped behind Ty.

Palmer looked around. "Hey, there's Sawyer and Ty. They're pulling in from the wrong side of town. Maybe they went over to see Ford. Think Sawyer said they were out there earlier this week, too." He turned back to her. "Hold your shirt up so we can see what it looks like."

Louise did a fast shuffle in her hands so the words were pointed in and held the shirt to her chest. "It's perfect. Thanks so much for thinking of me. Don't let me hold you up anymore."

"I told you, you're not holding me up. Relax, Louise."

Sawyer and Ty walked toward them. Less than twenty feet away.

She grabbed the bag from Palmer and shoved the shirt in. "I need to go check on Tella."

"She's fine. She just went to the restroom. It's Patty's Diner. She knows the way and will be out in a minute." He took a hold of her arm. "What's the matter with you? I've never seen you act this way."

Louise's panicked eyes flew from Palmer's chest to Sawyer and, finally, to Ty. He was smiling like he was glad to see her. It faded as her expression couldn't be forced into anything remotely resembling happiness.

This situation could not get any worse.

"Mommy! Mommy!" Tella came running out of Patty's.

"Don't run in the diner," Louise said automatically.

"I'm not in the diner, I'm out of it," Tella backtalked, which she seldom did, but it just made the slow-motion horror film that had started to unroll before Louise's eyes all the more real. "I forgot to tell you what Uncle Palmer said."

Palmer let go of her arm and bent down to get more level with Tella. "What did I say, honey?"

Tella rushed on, but Louise didn't hear. With Palmer leaning down, she could clearly see the stunned expression on Ty's face. His eyes flew to hers. She couldn't pull hers away from him, couldn't get her mouth to move, couldn't get any sound to come out of her mouth at all.

Behind her, Ames gasped, but Louise barely noticed. Ty's eyes flew from her to Tella, back to her, then back to Tella. He took a step closer, his hand out. But he stopped and dropped it. The bewildered expression on his face was swept away by thunderclouds of anger. Louise stepped back, her hand going to her throat.

Palmer had turned his head at Ames's gasp, and now he straightened, his eyes going from Ames to Louise to Ty. They hooked on Ty and stayed there.

Beside Palmer, Sawyer had figured out that something was going on as he scanned Ames's face then Palmer's. He looked at Louise. Then Tella. Then Ty. His gaze, too, latched onto Ty's face and didn't move.

Tella, finally figuring out that no one was listening to her and that something was very, very wrong, faded off into silence.

Long, drawn-out seconds of silence passed. Louise wasn't sure who moved first, Palmer or Sawyer, but her brothers seemed to figure everything out at the exact same second.

They turned on Ty, who didn't even look at them. His gaze was stuck on Tella, anger still on his face.

Louise could remember only a few times in their adult life when her brothers had gotten angry. They were both even-tempered and fairly laid-back. Sawyer was a bit more of a commander than Palmer, but neither were fighters. But, like they'd planned it, they each grabbed two fistfuls of Ty's t-shirt and slammed him against Patty's Diner. Thankfully, they missed the window by about four inches.

Sawyer cursed, calling Ty names that Louise had never heard. Palmer's face was as red as blood, and veins stood out on his neck. The muscles in his arms bulged as they held Ty off his feet and against the building.

Ty had been in his share of fistfights. Louise had actually seen him fight on TV, not that they saw all his games. And he was big. But so were her brothers. Strong cowboys whose muscles were earned taming the tough North Dakota flatlands and forcing a living from it.

But Ty didn't look scared. He didn't even seem to notice the men holding him, yelling in his face. His jaw had tightened. His eyes narrowed. His entire face was dark with his brows drawn to a point above his nose.

"I've waited nine years to put my fist through his face," Sawyer growled in a mountain lion tone.

"I've waited just as long," Palmer said in a tone that matched it.

Their tirade stopped as they gasped for air.

Into the first breath of silence since they'd grabbed Ty, Tella's little-girl voice floated like an angel's wings. "Uncle Palmer, Uncle Sawyer, is that...is that Ty Hanson, the hockey forward?" She stepped toward them tentatively, whether because of her uncles' wrath or because she couldn't believe Ty actually stood in front of her. She pointed to her shirt. "*This* Ty Hanson?"

Palmer and Sawyer turned to look at their niece. They looked at each other, then as one, they looked back at Louise. "Say the word, sister."

"You know, you're not really holding him," Tella pointed out. Her face held the little-girl intelligent look that she used to recite interesting facts she learned in school. "His arms are hanging down. I think he could beat you up if he really wanted to." She stepped closer. "Please let him go. If you're nice to him, maybe he'd teach me how to play hockey."

Ty's eyes squeezed tight before his jaw clenched even harder. When they opened, they were tortured. "Holy frig, Louise. How could you do this to me?"

Louise's chest felt like it ripped down the middle. Pain like she'd never experienced before spread out in waves from the center. Her head hung down. She was the worst person in the world. She was only trying to do the best thing, the right thing, and it had backfired like a bomb in her face. "I'm sorry." Her voice cracked.

Her brothers loosened their grip, and Ty slid down the diner exterior.

"You didn't know," Palmer spoke to Ty with wonder in his voice.

"You didn't tell him?" Sawyer asked Louise in a half-whisper.

Louise lifted her head. Her eyes were burning, and her chest thumped with pain, but apparently, she could still feel anger because it blazed in dark shades of red across her vision. "This is why I was in a big rush for you to leave. My entire life has just exploded and is lying in a big mess in front of me. I want you two to just leave. Get out of here. I need to talk to my daughter."

Louise took several shaky breaths. She never spoke to her brothers like that.

Ty hissed, and his cheeks bulged, but his lips pressed together. If she had to guess, she would have said that he was going to correct her. Tella wasn't *her* daughter. She was *their* daughter.

Chapter 13

He had a daughter.

Louise had a child.

A little girl. His little girl. The kid didn't even know about him, that he was her dad, and she was wearing his jersey.

He'd never felt like this in his whole life. Like his head was going to explode. Like his chest was a whirlpool at flood stage, with everything swirling and moving, pieces and parts hitting against each other.

He barely noticed Louise's brothers leaving. If someone had done to Georgia what he'd done to Louise, he might not have left the guy standing when he walked away.

Her brothers hadn't known who the father was. Louise must not have told anyone.

His heart heaved as he thought of her alone and pregnant. She had another year of high school. That would have been torture walking the halls. Maybe she didn't even graduate.

He'd been oblivious. His mother had never said a word. Not a single word. She had to have known about Louise being pregnant and having a baby, but anytime she'd related the gossip of Sweet Water, Louise had been absent, other than mentioning she was valedictorian. His mother had said that much. Ty had always been listening for her name. He just figured Louise had left.

His breath was shaky, and he felt like he was having an out-of-body experience, hovering above himself and looking down on his shocked and quaking body.

Louise had her hand on Tella's shoulder. There were tears on her cheeks. How many times had she cried, because of him, and he hadn't been there?

Tella was silent beside her. Her face was serious and an almost perfect replica of Louise. Except she had his darker blue eyes and the cleft in his chin. Her hair was his shade of darker brown rather than Louise's golden blond.

Vaguely, he heard Palmer's pickup pull away with the stock trailer. Sawyer had walked down the street toward the park.

"Why was everyone yelling?" Tella asked.

Louise swiped at her eyes. "Everyone is okay. I just have some things I need to say to this man."

This man? He stepped forward but stopped short at Louise's look. It wasn't a heated look. More like pleading.

"Can I still go to Uncle Sawyer's house, even though you yelled at him?"

"I'm sorry. I shouldn't have yelled. And I'll apologize to Uncle Sawyer. And yes, you can go. School starts next week, and this is the last time you'll be able to stay for a while."

"Mommy?"

"Yes, dear?"

Tella slanted a look at Ty. "Do you know Mr. Hanson? Like, he's a hockey player on TV, but he's from our town. Right? You know him?"

"Yes."

"Is he...good?"

"Yes."

Tella closed the few feet between them, her little hand held out, her face a mixture of seriousness and suppressed excitement. "I'm Tella, and I've seen you on TV."

He closed his eyes and drew a breath before he bent down, taking her hand in his. "I'm Ty, and maybe I'll get to see you again."

Tella's lips moved up in a little smile. "Maybe."

She turned abruptly. "I love you, Mommy. Can I go with Uncle Sawyer now?"

"Yes," Louise said, her voice sounding pained.

He wanted to throttle her and hold her at the same time. She'd had a baby, *his baby*, by herself.

Tella took off, running down the sidewalk, her backpack bouncing on her back, toward Sawyer, who stood, leaning against a light pole, hands in his pockets, several blocks down. His casual stance didn't fool Ty. The man was angry, and although he'd given them the privacy Louise had asked for, he'd not gone out of sight. Sawyer bent down and caught Tella as she flung herself into his arms.

Louise's brothers had stepped in and filled the void that Ty had left.

Sawyer helped Tella into his old truck, throwing her backpack in the bed, before climbing in and giving Louise one last searching look. Louise lifted her hand. Tella waved back. Sawyer jerked his head. His pickup pulled out and rumbled by, with Sawyer giving Ty one last, hard look.

Louise stood in front of him, her head down, her hands clasped in front of her, her fingers twisting. Like she was waiting for him to unleash on her.

In a way, yeah, he was angry. But part of him, the bigger part, was aghast at what Louise had been through, what she'd given up, what she'd had to do. All because of him.

And another part of him had already realized if she hadn't done what she did, if she hadn't kept her mouth shut and sucked it up and had their baby by herself, he wouldn't be a professional hockey player, one of the best in the league.

He didn't know why she didn't tell him. Maybe that had nothing to do with it, but he couldn't have been a father, and maybe a husband, and still accomplished what he had. Just wouldn't have happened.

He owed Louise.

"Why?" It was the first word he could get past his constricted throat, coming out in a scratchy whisper. "Why?"

She squared her shoulders and looked up. "This was my secret."

"Obviously."

Her lips didn't even twitch. "Of course, I didn't know I was pregnant until you'd been gone a month."

That's right. He'd stayed less than a week for his dad's funeral and left without talking to her again, but she wouldn't have known then, anyway. It was that last night, the night he'd fought with his dad, when he'd allowed his emotions to control him, and they'd gotten sucked into the void of heat and lust. Only that night. And he'd never spoken to her again. He couldn't believe she was even talking to him.

She hadn't said anything more, so he made his mouth move. "I know. There was only the one night."

She nodded and looked away. Embarrassed, probably. But she didn't need to be. Not for him. There hadn't been another moment in his life that he'd relived so often or with such longing. She'd been beautiful. Sweet. And had ruined him for anyone else.

Louise shoved her hands in her jean's pockets. "There was never a question about whether I was going to have her. And I always wanted to keep her. But even at seventeen, I knew that I'd have to give up a lot."

"I would have helped." He grabbed his hat in consternation before lifting it and shoving his hand through his hair.

"At the time, I thought if you'd have called, I would have told you. But I don't think I would have." She looked up at him, her clear blue eyes meeting his. "I knew you would have to sacrifice, too. And I know that was a choice that you could make for yourself—how much you wanted to sacrifice—but I didn't want to be your ball and chain."

He didn't want to scare her, and he didn't want her to run, but his arms ached. He stepped forward, taking her upper arms in his hands. "You're not. You wouldn't have been."

"When you didn't call, and didn't call, and didn't call, and never came home, I couldn't think anything else. Honestly, after you disappeared without contacting me, I didn't want to tell you. I didn't want you to be a part of my life only because I had your baby. I wanted you to want me for me. Or not at all." She clenched her jaw, her head tilted way back to look up into his face. "I know you had the right to be involved with your child, and I took your choice from you. I deprived Tella of a father, and I made the easiest choice for myself."

She was so beautiful to him, and she was hurting so badly. He could hardly stop himself from wrapping her up in his arms. "No one knew—your brothers didn't even know—that I was the father?"

"No one. I didn't tell a soul."

"Why not?" he asked, but he was almost certain of the answer.

"People might have made you come back. You might have been pressured, if not to marry me, then to pay child support. How could you do that?"

He couldn't have. He would have had to quit hockey and get a job that actually paid something. He'd have done it, though. He knew he would have. His dad's guilt would have been hanging around his neck, and hockey would have become the penance. Louise had made sure that didn't happen.

"Everything I am, who and what I am, is because of what you did. What you sacrificed." He couldn't fight it anymore and moved his hands from her arms, putting his own arms around her and pulling her into his. She stiffened, and his heart stuttered. Then she relaxed, leaning her head against his chest and pressing her body against his. He closed his eyes against the sweet torture of having Louise in his arms again. He could hardly keep his hands still, wanting to run them over her back and through her hair, feel the curve of her hip and the changes nine years had brought.

But he didn't.

He froze as her hands tentatively touched his waist. His breath blew out harshly as they slipped around, burning his sides and back.

The fire that had burned so brightly between them years ago burned even hotter now. He couldn't let it consume them again. Not after what Louise had been through after the first time.

So he didn't lower his head like he wanted, needed, to, didn't wait for her face to turn up, didn't touch his lips to hers like he longed to do. He didn't lift her up, dragging her body up his and giving him better access to her mouth and cheeks and neck.

He didn't do any of those things he hungered to do but just stood on the sidewalk and held the woman who had made his professional hockey career possible.

He tamped down all his other thoughts and tried to focus. "I owe you."

"No."

"Yes. We both know you paid and I didn't."

"It was always my choice."

He didn't want to fight. Not now. "I'd like to know my daughter."

"She's your biggest fan."

"That you didn't raise her to hate me is a miracle I can't even be-lieve." His voice was rough. How had Louise watched her daughter wear his jersey, listened to her talk about him, and not hated it?

Her eyes were clear and honest. "I couldn't do that. But I didn't push her toward you, either. She chose you."

He stepped back, putting distance he didn't want between them, running his hands down her arms as they dropped from his waist, and grabbing her hands. "You could have influenced her, and you know it. I'm thankful for your restraint." His eyes searched hers. "Be with me tonight. When you get off work, be with me." He was begging, and he didn't care.

Her mouth opened then closed. "I promised Paul we'd go see what-ever movie is playing at the theater tonight."

His throat closed in something like panic. He couldn't lose her. Not when he'd just gotten her back. Not when she fit even better in his arms than she had the first time. He wanted to crowd her, stalk her, make her choose him, but that would only push her away. So he dropped her hands and stepped back farther. Suddenly he felt like watching a movie at the old theater tonight, too.

"I'm not going to quit chasing you. I wasn't after you to begin with because we have a child together." Those words sent a buzz down his spine. "But I can't deny that ups the stakes for me. I don't know my daughter at all. I don't want another man raising her."

She lifted her chin, and he knew he'd pushed too hard. So he backed off. "I do get to see her, right?"

Her face relaxed into something like regret. "She's yours, too."

He stared at her, shaking his head. "I'm sorry. I just can't believe it. You and me, together, in another little person. That's so amazing. She has your face."

"And your eyes."

"Your seriousness."

"And your coordination."

His head snapped up. "She's good at sports?"

Louise gave a soft smile. "She's just eight. But yeah, she's good at everything she does."

"I want to teach her everything."

"She already loves you."

"I want to get to know her. Even if you do choose Paul." He stumbled over his name.

"You can." Louise looked away. "I was afraid you might try to take her from me. I know you have more resources than I do."

"Never. No. I promise you—"

She raised a brow. He'd broken so many promises.

"I'll put it in writing. We can get a court order that you have sole custody. I would never do that. But I want her. I want to know the little person that we've created." He wanted, more than anything, for them to be a family. Which was weird, because until the last hour, he'd not even been sure he'd wanted kids or a family. All he wanted was Louise. Now, he wanted Louise and their child.

She pulled her phone out of her pocket. "Oh my. It's time for my shift. I have to go in."

"Louise?"

She stopped in the act of turning, her face a question.

"You don't have to work."

A thin, white line appeared between her pressed lips. "I don't want this, me, to become about money for you."

His back teeth ground together. "I'm trying to figure out what you want. To be frank, I'm confused." He pushed his hat more firmly on his head. "I'll see you around." He turned and walked blindly away, not thinking about where he was going. How could he?

He wanted to be with Louise. She wanted Paul.

He wanted to ease her burden with money; she didn't want it.

Whatever he tried to offer, she refused.

Chapter 14

Louise pocketed the tip and swiped at the table. Her shift seemed to drag on at a snail's pace. She'd barely been working an hour when Ty had walked in and sat down at his regular booth in the corner. Looked like he'd worked out and showered, since he was wearing a different shirt and his hair was slightly damp.

Like their conversation wasn't fresh enough in her mind, she couldn't shake the amazing feeling of being held in his arms again. The feeling of safety and comfort. Peace. And the heat. She'd forgotten all about that heat that consumed a person, body and soul. It was constantly there with Ty, exploding into open flames when he touched her.

He'd ordered a hamburger and fries, but he wasn't really eating, his eyes tracking her wherever she went. She could feel them like a physical touch. She supposed it should feel creepy or stalkerish, but it made her feel desirable. Beautiful, even. Like she had control and could move them where she wished. It made her want to go over and touch his cheek. Feel his stubble against her hand. Push him back against the booth, knowing he'd go, that he'd open his mouth for her kiss and allow her whatever she wanted. There was a puissant pull in that knowledge. That he'd give her anything she wanted because he couldn't resist her.

But she was a mother now. Tella had to come first. Even if, once Tella knew about her father, she decided she wanted him more than the mother who had sacrificed everything to raise her.

That's the main reason she'd still sent Tella with Sawyer. Yes, she needed to come clean with Ty, and they needed to present a united front, but she couldn't compete with a hockey star. When Tella found out that he was her father, why would she want to have to continue to stay with her boring, overworked, constantly tired mother?

At a little after five, Paul came in. Louise stood by Ty's table and had just asked him if he wanted more water or dessert. He saw Paul first. And stiffened. She could almost see his hackles raising.

Paul walked over and sat against the other wall, his face placid and sweet. Even-tempered. Unruffled. Steady as a rock. That was Paul.

Maybe it was because she'd been working for the last hour under Ty's hot stare, but Louise noticed that Paul gave her a short smile and wave before sliding into his seat. He cared, at least she thought he did, but he wasn't consumed with her.

Ty seemed to look at her either because he wanted to or because he couldn't do anything else when she was in the room.

She felt a little bad comparing the two, but how could she not?

She took Paul's order, and when his food came out, she took her break, like she always did, sitting across from him. She realized she hadn't talked to him since the last day she'd worked. She hadn't thought of him once and didn't really care what he was doing. He probably had the same thoughts and feelings about her.

It wasn't a love match. So that made sense. If they got married, in time they would grow to care about each other. Paul's most appealing quality was his amazingness with Tella. He was great with her. He'd be a fabulous dad. He already helped with her school projects.

Then there was his steadiness. He'd never leave her. He was calm and rational and would allow her to do whatever she wanted with her money, which was the reason she'd asked him to marry her in the first place.

"You couldn't find that ring?"

Louise jerked a startled glance at Paul before looking at her finger, like she wasn't sure if there was a ring on it or not. "Um, actually, I didn't even look for it." She gave him an apologetic smile. "We've been busy putting vegetables up this week and had some drama with Tella this afternoon."

It wasn't exactly "with" Tella, but close enough.

"Oh, okay." He spooned mashed potatoes into his mouth. "If you can't find it, let me know. I can go get something. I was just surprised by your offer and didn't want to go get something you wouldn't like."

"Thanks. I'll let you know." She didn't dare look over to the corner where Ty sat, but she could feel his eyes burning into the side of her head.

She squirmed a little, just realizing she should probably tell Paul that Tella's father was in town. It'd be best if he heard it from her. Tonight. She'd tell him at the movie because there was no way she could tell him with Ty staring at her like he was.

"I'd better get back to work. It's busy in here tonight."

"Yeah, okay. You meeting me at the theater at seven?"

"Yes." Usually she worked until closing time, but on Friday nights, Patty, who was back from her vacation, came in because they had a floating close. They might not shut down right at eight o'clock if there were still patrons coming in.

Her back ached, and her feet were tired. But as she stood, and Paul gave her a kind smile, she suddenly saw with clarity—she couldn't marry Paul. She couldn't do that to him. It wasn't fair. She didn't love him and never would. Ty would always be between them. She'd have to live without the money.

When she looked over, Ty was talking on his phone. She took care of her other customers and finally started over to his table. But he'd left. Great. Did he not pay for his meal?

But as she got closer, she could see that there was a green bill lying on the table. A hundred. She put a hand to her forehead and rubbed. What was she going to do? She reached the table and could see there was writing on the napkin under the bill. "Keep the change. -T"

Her heart flipped. If he hadn't signed his initial, she'd suspect that he did this a lot wherever he went. But while Ty might be a sports superstar, he was raised as frugally as she was, and she doubted he threw hundred-dollar bills around. Maybe he'd done it because of Tella. Because he felt he owed Louise. Or maybe he'd done it because he wanted to do something nice for her, because he liked her. She liked that idea best.

TY STOPPED HIS CAR in the lot by the park at the end of the street. Where he'd walked with Louise just a couple of nights ago. It felt like years had passed. He turned to the passenger seat. "Hold on. I'll open your door."

"I'm your sister, not your girlfriend." Georgia laughed.

"You're my date for tonight. Let me get it." He walked around and opened her door. She stepped out with a smile still on her face, her wild hair only partially tamed in some kind of sloppy knot on top of her head. She wore jeans and cowgirl boots that would probably fit Tella and a button-down western shirt that she had tucked in. Dangly earrings hung in her ears.

Her head came to the middle of his chest. He'd forgotten how small she was. He could see how she might be mistaken for a twelve-year-old. That, combined with the fact that she was holed up on the ranch with Ford, made him wonder if she'd ever get married.

After closing the door, he offered her his arm, and she laughed as she took it. They strolled up the street, taking their time, talking about the things they remembered from their youth.

He hadn't told her he was a father. He'd barely processed the information himself. But he assumed Louise would want to wait until she told Tella, so Ty closed his mouth over his big news and made small talk with his sister.

He'd not thought about taking Georgia to the movie until he'd visited Ford and her and realized that it'd been years since he spent any time at all with his siblings. Ford had declined his invitation, and Georgia said it'd been years since he'd been off his ranch, but Georgia had taken him up on it.

He found he was enjoying her company, but he was unprepared for her next question.

"So why are you really taking me tonight?"

Guilt pressed on him as he looked down into her laughing eyes which were such a dark hazel as to be almost brown.

"I really realized that it's been years since we did anything other than you coming to see me with Mom."

"And?" Her brows were dark against her fair complexion, and she'd always been able to arch just one way up. She did that now.

He couldn't pretend. "And a girl I have my eye on is going with another guy tonight. I thought it would be too stalkerish if I just went by myself, and I wanted to spend time with you anyway."

"Perfect. We need a plan." Georgia didn't miss a beat, like she did this every day.

"A plan?"

She shrugged. "Sure. We'll make her jealous."

"She knows you're my sister."

"Oh. Yeah. I guess the plan should start with me knowing her name." She gave a giggle. It was nice to be out with a girl who didn't feel like she needed to act perpetually bored. Or be on her phone constantly. Even if Georgia was his sister.

He hesitated. He assumed the theater wouldn't be full. Georgia might figure it out on her own. But if he told her, she knew about Tella, and she might figure that out too.

"Louise."

Her eyes opened wide. "That's why you're back! You guys met somewhere—" She stopped abruptly and tilted her head to the side. "But Louise never goes anywhere. How did you—" She stopped again; he could see her mind working, powerless to stop it.

"You're the father," she whispered, dawning realization coloring her tone. "It's you. You're the one who got her pregnant and left. Disappeared..." She thought back again. "Dad died. You left. She was pregnant in school that year."

He hated the look in her eyes as she looked up at him, half disbelief, half accusation. "It was you."

"Yes." Guilt gripped Ty's throat in a choking grip.

Her hand came up and covered her mouth. "Oh, wow." She slanted a look at him. "I hated that person. Louise was so alone. She'd never had a boyfriend. She didn't even talk to guys, and there she was pregnant. Obviously, the guy didn't even like her enough to stick around after he got what he wanted."

"That's not true!" he cried.

"That's what all the kids were saying. If I were her, I would have quit school, but she suffered through it every day." Georgia shook her head. "Sorry. It's not my job to make you feel guilty. It's just that for-ever I've harbored a special dislike for the jerk who took advantage of Louise."

"I didn't take advantage of her!" Ty rubbed the back of his neck. Had he taken advantage of her?

"That's not what it looked like." Georgia sighed. "To me, anyway, because I admired Louise. She was a little older than me, but I worked with her in chorus some in a small group setting. She was the pianist, and she was smart and funny. She was always early and stayed until the last person had practiced and never complained. I admired that."

He'd been wrapped up in sports and had no clue what the music department was doing.

"Yeah, I admired her too."

"I never even saw you two together."

"No." They had almost reached the theater. Louise and Paul were nowhere in sight. Maybe they were already in.

"And?"

"I snuck out to meet her."

"Why? She was a good girl. Dad and Mom would have approved if you wanted to date her." Georgia sounded truly confused, and he figured he owed her at least the basics. He didn't want his sister hating him. Or thinking less of Louise.

"It started that Peggy got Louise to meet me to tell me that Peggy wanted to break up with me. The breakup didn't bother me. I wasn't in love with Peggy or anything close. Louise met me at the river, and I just asked her to meet me again. And again. I was falling for her, and I guess I wanted to keep it to myself. It was our special time and place. At first. Then I started thinking about not going to college and giving up hockey to stay with her, and I knew how that would go over with Dad. So, then, yeah, it became sneaking, and I truly didn't want anyone to know. When I finally talked to Dad, he was furious. We fought. But, honestly, with Louise, it was about me wanting to stay with her and not go to college. Our relationship was innocent. All we did was talk and kiss."

Georgia raised that arched brow. "I know I'm your little sister, but I grew up on a ranch. I've got the boy-girl thing figured out. Tella didn't get here from you two talking and kissing."

"Right. The last night was the only night we did anything I would be ashamed to tell our parents about."

Georgia sighed. "I guess no one ever knew anything about you two." She shrugged. "I didn't suspect, but because she never said anything, it really did look bad on whoever left her like that."

"I'm not saying I was a saint. I made promises to her that I didn't keep. It's complicated, and I don't want to get into it, but I never 'took what I wanted' from Louise. But everything else is my fault."

Georgia was silent for a moment. "Okay, so I've seen her with Paul the last while back. I assume that's who she's going to be with tonight?"

"Yeah."

"I'm sorry, big brother, but if you can't out-man Paul, I can't help you." She grinned, and he rolled his eyes.

"I lied to her. I didn't keep my word. I left her and never called. She doesn't trust me."

Georgia gave him a level look. "If someone had done that to me, you wouldn't be encouraging me to go back with them."

"I know." His chest deflated. "Everyone is against me. Everyone, except I think Louise might like me a little."

"Tella's your biggest fan. She wears your jersey everywhere."

"I can't use our daughter as leverage. I just need time to prove that I'm better than what I was when I left her."

"You're leaving again when the season starts."

"I am. Maybe she'll come with me." It wasn't something he'd even thought about until the words were out of his mouth. But, hey, why not? Tella and Louise could be close to him. They could come to his games. He'd find a place for them to stay.

"Good luck with that. Louise loves North Dakota."

They didn't speak anymore as Ty opened the door and Georgia walked through. He purchased tickets for the movie that was showing that night, plus popcorn and drinks. They walked into the dimly lit theater room.

His eyes picked Louise out immediately, even from behind. Her long hair was in a braid, which hung over the back of her seat. Paul and she sat about in the middle row, with Paul on the end seat doing something on his phone.

Georgia must have seen them too, because she led them right to the seat behind them and sat down one seat in. "I don't know why I'm helping you with this, other than you're a good man and she deserves better than that," Georgia whispered in his ear.

"That's the best you can do? 'You're a good man?'" he whispered back.

Georgia giggled. "Well, you did toss me in the creek that once. I need revenge."

"Come on. Everyone likes to go swimming."

"It was January."

They laughed together. And then he argued because he couldn't let his little sister win. "No, it wasn't. The creek would have been frozen solid by then. It was probably only October. Possibly November."

"In North Dakota, that's cold." She shivered and ran her hands up her arms like she was still remembering how cold it had been.

They talked and laughed until the movie started. He'd forgotten how much fun he'd had with his siblings. Too bad Ford wouldn't come. Too bad Georgia felt like she was stuck helping Ford. He wished he could talk her out of it and into doing something else with her life. But Ford seemed to need her.

The movie started. It was an action movie with a subplot of romance and bits of humor. There was lots of blowing things up which seemed to hit Paul's funny bone every time, since he laughed at each blast.

Ty had settled more comfortably with his ankle resting on his knee and his arm lying behind Georgia's backrest. Every once in a while, they shared a laugh or a comment. He was actually having a great time, when, about halfway through the movie, Louise got up, tapping Paul's arm, then slipped out.

Georgia looked at him in question. He shrugged but lifted his arm off the armrest and straightened his legs, thinking to go after her, since Paul had barely glanced away from the movie.

Georgia put a hand on his arm. "Let me," she whispered.

He stood so she could get out, wanting to follow but knowing it was probably Louise going to the ladies' room or something, and he was already being a stalker by going to the movie he knew she was going to and sitting right behind her.

Chapter 15

Louise leaned over the sink, staring at her reflection in the mirror. Ty had sat behind her. She'd recognize his voice anywhere. And he had some giggling, squeaky little thing with him. Happy and bubbly. The kind of girl he deserved. But she didn't have to sit there and be tortured the whole movie while her "date" laughed at the gore and ignored her.

She slapped the sink. She was being unfair to Paul. Lots of people loved that movie. It was a huge hit nationwide. Paul was a nice guy, and he didn't deserve what she was doing to him—comparing him to Ty and finding him lacking in every way.

The door opened, and Louise started looking in the mirror at her eye like she had something in it and wishing she'd gone into a stall. She didn't think she'd get company.

"Louise?" a familiar voice asked. Familiar in that it had been behind her and beside Ty the whole movie.

She glanced in the mirror. "Georgia?" He'd taken his sister to the movie? All the jealousy that had beaten its way up her throat withered away. She straightened, her attitude doing a complete turnaround with this development.

"I saw you leave, just wanted to make sure everything was okay." Georgia touched her shoulder. "And we keep saying we'll catch up, but we never do."

Louise turned and hugged Georgia. "I'm fine. I didn't realize it was you behind me, but I recognized Ty's voice."

Georgia's left brow arched. One side of her mouth moved up, just a little. "Ty told me he was coming because you would be here." She held

Louise's eyes with a steady gaze. "That's the first I'd ever heard anything about Ty and you. I guessed the rest."

It took a few seconds for Louise to realize Georgia was talking about Tella. Her eyes widened. "Please don't say anything. Tella doesn't know. I am almost certain she'll be fine with it; she adores Ty, but..."

Georgia held up her hand. "I won't say a word. Not until you've told Tella." She paused. "But when are you going to do that?"

Louise shrugged. "She's at Sawyer's right now." A shadow of something passed over Georgia's face. But her bright smile returned. Louise wasn't sure what that meant, so she kept going. "I figured I'd tell her when she got home."

"So, Ty's pretty serious about you."

"He's been away for almost a decade. That's not serious. Plus, he has his choice of women. Once he leaves, he'll forget all about me."

"There are a lot of women, but never anyone special. I think I know why, now."

Louise looked away. The flower basket on the small table by the hand towels had been there since she was little. Faded but familiar.

"You can't really be serious about Paul? I mean, Paul is really nice and everything, but he's, what, fifteen years older than you? And, well, I know my opinion is biased, but seriously? If I had to choose between Paul and Ty, Ty is the easy win."

Louise had been under so much pressure, searching her soul, wanting to do the best thing for her daughter, but not wanting to make decisions based on money. She'd known Georgia since they were young. Georgia would keep her secret.

"I got a letter." She gave Georgia the rundown of the letter—that she would inherit one billion dollars if she got married before Christmas.

"Oh, wow." Georgia's eyes had gotten big and almost bugged out of their sockets. "But that's perfect! Marry Ty."

"Whoa. First of all, he hasn't asked. Secondly, he just showed up. Last time he made promises to me, he disappeared and didn't even call. I have a child to consider and will not allow that to happen again. And, third, I don't really know him."

"You do too. You grew up with him. You knew him from church and school. Yeah, he's a big hockey star now, but he's still Ty. He's honest. He works hard, and he's head over heels for you."

"Paul lives in North Dakota."

"Our mother has a ranch in North Dakota," Georgia said with her brows raised.

"She's selling."

Georgia's face dimmed. "I know." Her eyes brightened. "Maybe Ty will buy it."

"Maybe I will buy it." That had been the plan.

"You're serious."

"Yes. I was." She leaned a hip against the sink. "That's what I wanted to do with my billion. But I've already decided I can't marry Paul."

Georgia smiled wide.

"I'd be using him, and it wouldn't be right. I know he likes me, like a friend, and when I offered marriage, he agreed. Maybe to be nice. I don't know. I need to talk to him."

"I don't think I'll tell Ty this."

Louise laughed. "It's up to you. I'll probably tell him the next time I see him. That I won't marry Paul. Not about the money."

"Not tonight?"

"No."

"You know, he threw me into the creek when I was little, and I might just have to tease him with scenarios about you and Paul and what you're doing after the movie."

Louise held her hands up. "I have nothing to do with that."

"Nope. Sibling torture." She hooked an arm through Louise's. "It was good to see you. Wish we could get together more often, but Ford is so demanding."

"You're working for him?" She pushed the bathroom door open, and they both stepped out.

"Yeah, as kind of a housekeeper, business planner, event organizer."

"I thought he didn't go anywhere."

"He doesn't. I do it for him." Georgia rolled her eyes like that explained everything. "It's too much, and I've told him he needs to hire someone else, but he won't listen. He wants me to do it all."

"Then I guess you need to quit."

"Oh." Georgia stopped with her hand on the theater room door. "I never thought of that." She pulled the door open, and they walked in.

AFTER THE MOVIE WAS over, Louise stood up with Paul. She fiddled with her purse and tried to take up a little time, trying to avoid having to talk to Ty, but Paul got pulled along with the crowd and started walking out without her.

She turned to follow him but from behind her, Ty said, "Let him go. He doesn't deserve you."

Louise gave him a dark look and continued to walk, afraid if she stopped, she'd want to be with Ty rather than the man she'd come with.

Catching up to Paul at the door, she said, a little breathlessly, "I need to talk to you."

"That's fine. You can walk me to my apartment. It's only three blocks away."

She did not want to go there. Paul had been nothing but a gentleman, and she was sure that's all he had in his mind tonight, but she wasn't going to his apartment.

He looked around at the night sky. "It's not too cold out tonight. You'll be fine."

"Okay." She didn't want Ty to come out and see them arguing. They started down the sidewalk. "Thanks so much for going to the movie." She'd ended up paying for their tickets, but that was probably an accident on his part because he'd gone to the restroom while they were in line.

"No problem."

"I need to talk to you."

"Okay."

He'd never been super talkative. It hadn't bothered her before.

She took a deep breath and braced herself, even though she knew she wasn't going to be breaking his heart. "I know it was my idea to get married and I gave you that offer, but I've changed my mind. I think it would probably work, but I don't think it would be fair to you." Hundreds more reasons rushed to her tongue, but she held them back.

Paul stopped walking. "A deal's a deal."

"You don't love me," Louise said softly. They weren't far enough away from the movie theater for there to be enough distance between her and Ty. For some reason, she didn't want him to hear this.

His brows knitted. His kind face held confusion. "Me loving you wasn't part of the deal."

"No, of course it's not." He didn't deny that he didn't love her. It should make this easier, but it really didn't.

He started walking again, slower. "This is a breach of contract."

"But we didn't sign anything! We're not married."

"But you said you would."

He was right; she'd given her word. She'd even been the one to make the offer. But she couldn't go through with it.

Paul sighed, a heavy sigh, like he was really being put out. "I guess the decision is yours and I can't make you, but maybe you should think things through better next time."

His eyes held hurt, and Louise hated that.

"I'm sorry." She would be doing him a worse disservice if she married him, but she wasn't going to get into it with him. "I guess I'll head back to my car." It was parked on the other end of the street.

Paul's soulful eyes looked at her, and she felt like she'd kicked a puppy. "I'll see you around," he said.

Louise closed her eyes before nodding and waving. She turned and walked away.

Everything inside of her wanted to protect Tella. All of her mother's instincts wanted to cover her child. Paul would have made a great dad.

But she'd made a mistake by propositioning Paul. To marry him would have been an even bigger mistake. Making the offer in the first place had been a dumb idea. Now she had to face his displeasure and betrayal as she stood up and undid the thing she never should have done to begin with.

She was so deep in thought that she didn't see Georgia and Ty sitting on a bench at the entrance to the park, eating ice cream, until she was almost on them. Too late to change course, even if she wanted to. Her car was parked not twenty yards away.

She smiled at them as she passed. A strained smile, but hopefully they didn't notice. How did she always manage to make such a jumble out of her life?

To make it worse, if Palmer hadn't solved the ranch's financial problems, she might still be tempted to marry Paul. Although all of her rebelled at that idea. Especially with Ty sitting right in front of her.

"Want to join us for some ice cream?" Ty called out.

Her automatic response was "no," but Tella was with Sawyer for the evening. Gram and Pap were in bed by this time. Palmer and Ames were probably enjoying a peaceful evening alone together. A shaft of loneliness cut through her.

Her gaze took in Ty and Georgia. They never really looked like siblings, but they still looked good together. Ty's handsome brown hair and blue eyes, his strong jaw and wide shoulders, plus his height, contrasted so nicely with Georgia's wild, dark curly hair and her curvy but petite frame. Although it did kind of look like Ty was taking his daughter out and not his sister. Georgia looked so young.

"I don't want to interrupt sibling time together."

"I've spent enough time with him for one day," Georgia said. "Come on over, you'll keep us from killing each other."

"What kind of ice cream do you want? I'll go get you some." Ty flashed straight white teeth, and Louise couldn't look away.

She stopped. "You sure you don't mind?"

"We'd love to have you," Georgia said, standing. She closed the distance between them and linked her arm with Louise's. "Just for an ice cream."

Louise quit fighting herself and said, "Okay. I'll take vanilla."

"They whipped up a special batch of oatmeal cookie explosion," Ty said. "Sure you don't want to try it?" He held up his cone. "It's pretty good."

"No thanks." She'd gone out on a limb with Paul. It had just ended badly, and she didn't need to veer off the beaten path anytime again soon. Even with ice cream. "Vanilla is good."

"Okay." Ty hopped off the bench. The ice-cream store was just across the street. His shoulder brushed hers as he passed, and his eyes smiled.

She was glad he was so happy.

"What's wrong?" Georgia hissed as soon as he passed.

"I just told Paul I wasn't going to marry him and apologized for suggesting it in the first place."

"He was heartbroken?" Georgia said in such a disbelieving tone that Louise had to smile. Like, how could any man ever be heartbroken if Louise broke up with him?

"Thanks," Louise said dryly.

Georgia's head snapped around, and she looked at Louise for a few seconds before she understood. "Oh no! I didn't mean it like that."

"I know."

"I'm surprised you're upset about it, though. Are you having second thoughts?" Georgia led her to the bench, and they sat together.

"No. Nothing like that. He just seemed so down about it. I mean, he admitted he didn't love me, but he gave me guilt about breaking my word, and he was right. But marrying him wouldn't be fair to him. I didn't go into it, though." She bit her lip. "I know he would have been a steady dad for Tella, and I feel guilty. She's already lived most of her childhood with no dad, and it's all my fault."

Georgia cocked her head. "Not to flaunt Ty, because he is an annoying big brother, but maybe having a superstar hockey player for a dad will make it up to her a little?"

That was a perk, but it didn't make him a good dad. "Maybe."

Georgia bumped her shoulder. "And if you and Ty get together, that will stop all the tongues from wagging about anything else and focus on you and Ty."

"Yeah, until he leaves me again."

Georgia's smile dimmed. "He won't."

"My heart says you're right, but my brain points out that he's done it before. What if something happens to his mother? Or you? Or Ford? Would he leave me then? I mean, I don't expect him to put his summer fling above his dad, but maybe something would happen again that would put him in a position to have to choose between me and his family. I don't know what it could be, but something. You know?" Louise felt like she was whining, and she hated that feeling, but everything she'd said was the truth. Georgia had asked.

"I see what you're saying. You trust him, but you're not sure where you fit in order of importance. And if something happened, a fluke like

Dad passing away, you're not sure he wouldn't do the same thing again." Georgia crunched her cone, her eyes thoughtful.

"Exactly. And I know flukes don't happen very often. But they seem to work in my life a little more than average." She wrapped her arms around her waist. "I'm scared. I've already messed up so badly for Tella. I don't want to do it again. And yet, I almost did with Paul."

"Ty's only been home a few weeks. He needs to give you time." She gave a short nod then popped the rest of her cone into her mouth, but her eyes met Louise's. Both of them knew there wasn't much time.

Louise took a deep breath. "I need to trust him."

"You guys can work this out."

"You seem confident he even wants to."

"Mom and I have visited him several times a year. There are no girls in his life. Sure, you see pictures with women on his arm, but there's never been a steady girl. I told you, I really think that's because he's been stuck on you all this time."

"Maybe you're right."

Ty started back across the street with two cones in one hand and licking another. Georgia groaned. "Oh no. He got me another cone. I'm never going to be able to eat it all."

Louise laughed. "You have to. I'd feel weird if you two sit and watch me eat ice cream."

Georgia exaggerated squaring her shoulders. "Okay. I'll have to take one for the team, I guess."

Ty came back, holding the cones out for Georgia and Louise. "I've never taken two girls out at one time, so bear with me."

Georgia giggled. "I've never shared my date with someone else, so bear with me, too."

"I've never dated. So you can do whatever you want, and I'll think it's normal." Louise shrugged before licking the melting ice cream around the base of her cone. Maybe ice cream was sweeter when a man bought it for her. Or maybe it was just Ty.

Ty had stilled when she spoke, but he seemed to shake himself. "You just went to the movies with Paul. That counts."

"Does it count if I bought my own ticket?"

"No way!" Georgia almost shouted. "Most definitely not."

Ty studied Louise like he'd never seen her before. "You never dated?"

"Sweet Water isn't exactly a hotbed of romantic prospects, and my diaper bag didn't exactly scream 'sexy and available,' although I think it did attract certain guys who thought that since I'd already had a child, I was..." She let the sentence trail off, unwilling to finish. There hadn't been that many of those, anyway. Maybe two.

"Easy," Georgia supplied.

"Yes."

Ty's lips flattened. He looked like he was eating a lemon instead of ice cream. "Go out with me, Louise. On a date." His voice was rough like sand over gravel.

Maybe she'd shared too much. She hadn't wanted pity. She didn't want a pity date, either. "I haven't dated, but I do think it's rude to ask Date B out for another date while Date A is watching."

"Date A doesn't care. Date A is thrilled that Date C—is that how I'd refer to him in this scenario?—is finally getting his act together. He's slow. I'm warning you." Georgia's eyes danced.

Ty's look was dark and serious. "That wasn't a yes, Louise."

"How about let's meet to work on Harvest Fest?"

"Monday."

"We're canning corn in the morning."

"And you're resting after that."

She almost rolled her eyes. "Maybe if I'm sick."

"So we can talk about Harvest Fest while we work, and then you'll take a rest after we're done, before you come into the diner." Ty's ice cream dripped down the cone.

Louise pointed to it. "Your ice cream is melting."

"And you work too hard."

"It is necessary. I enjoy it."

Georgia kicked his cowboy boot. He slanted his gaze over at her while she made a cutting motion with her throat.

"I can see you guys." Louise licked her ice cream.

"Sometimes men are such idiots. He doesn't have the right to tell you what to do." Georgia rolled her eyes.

"I'm just trying to take care of her."

"She's been doing just fine by herself for the past nine years." Georgia gave him a telling look.

He shut his mouth.

"Thanks, Georgia. I appreciate the encouragement."

"You two make me want to pull my hair out," Ty growled before finishing off the rest of his ice-cream cone in one bite.

"You could date Paul. He doesn't backtalk," Louise suggested wryly, biting into her cone.

Ty swallowed. "Paul's a loser. He didn't deserve one second with you, let alone a whole movie."

At least Ty was good for her battered ego.

"Sometimes it's harder for a woman to survive than you think it is." Georgia held her cone out. "I can't finish this."

Ty took it from her. "Just what I wanted to hear." He licked around it then held it out to Louise. "Want some?"

For some reason, that question made tingles run down her fingers and up her spine, curling the hair on her neck. She stared at the ice cream where his tongue had just been. "No thanks," she squeaked out.

He took another lick. "Are you sure? It's the cookie explosion, and you might like it." He held it out to her, and after a slow second, her hand came up and took it.

Their fingers brushed. His were warm and hard, and the tingles from earlier came back with their friends, traveling up her arm, fogging her brain. Bringing the cone to her lips, she took a tentative lick. It was as good as he said. He took it back, and his eyes held hers as he turned the cone and licked over where she had.

"Whoo, it's getting hot out here." Georgia pretended to fan herself. "I think I'll just take a walk."

"No!" Louise ripped her eyes from Ty's, sticking the last of her own cone in her mouth. "Please don't. I need to get home." She stood up, taking a step to put some distance between them before she turned to Ty. "Thanks so much for the ice cream."

"Anytime," he said, low and sincere, like he was making a lifetime vow rather than a casual offer of ice cream.

"It was so nice to see you, Georgia." She took a breath and offered a smile. "Thanks for everything."

Ty straightened. "We'll follow you home."

"It's out of your way. Especially if you're taking Georgia home."

"I don't mind," Georgia piped up instantly.

"Humor me, please." Ty said softly.

She shrugged. It wasn't like they couldn't drive wherever they wanted. She could tell him no, and he'd probably listen. But he just wanted to make sure she was okay. After years of taking care of herself, she supposed she should love the fact that someone cared about her.

"Okay."

Chapter 16

Ty made it to Louise's house at 7:30 Monday morning. Palmer was just stepping off the porch with a bucket in each hand and a smile on his face. Ty didn't know too many men who smiled that early in the morning, but apparently Palmer was one of them. Most of the guys he knew grumbled about having to get out of bed before ten.

"'Morning, Ty. Louise said you were helping this morning." He handed Ty a bucket filled with sacks without a smile. "She also said that I wasn't allowed to touch you. She said things were a little more complicated than what they seemed. I trust Louise, but I've hated the guy who did this to her for a long time." He shook his head. "You were about the last person I would have guessed."

Well, there was no awkward, "you're a big hockey star, and I'm in awe of you" trash. That was actually refreshing.

Ty gave him a level look. "I would expect you to take care of your sister."

Palmer jerked his head. "If you need coffee, Louise has it going on the counter."

Tempted to grab a cup, just because he wanted to see Louise, he said, "Thanks, but I'm good. I drank some on the way here. It's a farmer's gasoline."

It was the right thing to say because Palmer laughed. "Pap always says that."

"My dad always said that."

Palmer's laugh died. "It's good you remember."

Ty lifted his chin in acknowledgment. How much different things would be if his dad had lived.

It took about an hour, but they had all the sacks that were in the buckets filled. Palmer carried three sacks in each hand. Ty imitated him, and soon they were all carried to the picnic table in the backyard by the garden.

As soon as Louise and Ames saw them outside, they came out with dishpans and started husking. Ty allowed his eyes to linger on Louise. She looked like she'd slept well. Her face was freshly scrubbed with pink cheeks under bright blue eyes. Her hair was back in a ponytail, and she wore sneakers with her jeans and t-shirt.

Palmer dropped his sacks and caught Ames up in a two-armed hug, planting a large kiss on her open lips.

She laughed and put her arms around him, kissing him back.

Ty wouldn't have said canning corn could be romantic or fun, but they seemed to make it both. His gaze skipped back to Louise. She was watching Palmer and Ames but seemed to feel his gaze, because her eyes turned to him.

If only he had the right to go over and kiss her. "Morning, beautiful," he said instead.

"Don't you have that backwards?" she asked with a little grin.

"Nope. Said exactly what I meant."

"'Morning, yourself."

He opened his mouth to say more, but Palmer slapped him on the shoulder. "One more trip and we should have everything here."

He gave Louise a last look before following her brother back out to the field. Then he helped husk corn until the first two dishpans were full.

Once the second pan was full, Louise stood up along with Ames. "Okay, we're going to go start."

"I'll help here until we're well ahead, then I have to go finish with the stock." Palmer indicated the picnic table and the full sacks of corn.

Ty wasn't really paying attention, though, because he was watching Louise as she walked in. He'd been hoping to spend time with her today, but it looked like he'd be outside and she'd be in.

Thirty minutes later, Palmer left to feed the stock. A half an hour after that, he walked out the back door with Ames following. "So, Ty, how would you feel about going in the kitchen to help out, so Ames can work out here with me?"

"I feel good about that," Ty said, standing up. He wouldn't need to be asked twice to go anywhere Louise was. "I'll carry this full pan of corn in."

Palmer gave him a steady look as they passed. Ty understood the warning in it but felt it was unnecessary. He had every honorable intention imaginable toward Louise.

Did that include marriage?

Ty stumbled on the step, catching himself before he dumped the entire pan of corn. He held it against his hip with one hand while he opened the door.

Did it?

Would he marry Louise?

What, exactly, were his intentions?

He wanted to be with her. He wanted to get to know his daughter. He wanted to hold Louise and protect her. Provide for her.

Did he want to spend the rest of his life with her? How would that look with hockey? How would they work that out with Tella?

He told himself to slow down, that he'd only been back a few weeks. There needed to be time. So, he'd enjoy her company and get to know her again, and she could get to know him.

But, yes, he knew for a certainty he had every intention of marrying Louise, no matter how they worked it out, if she would have him. As soon as she would have him.

He knew his mind. He knew the other girls that were out there, and none of them ever came close to not only making him feel like Louise made him feel but having her work ethic, her lack of guile, her dedication to her family, her self-sacrificial nature that would take the fall for something he'd done, so he could be successful. He'd be nuts to not want to make her his.

"THIS IS GOOD!" TY POPPED another hunk of corn kernels in his mouth.

"You're not supposed to be eating the fruit of our labor," Gram chided with a smile.

"I thought that's why we were doing this," Ty said incorrigibly.

Louise laughed, and Gram joined in. Louise couldn't remember having more fun canning corn, ever. She always looked forward to it. Sure, it was a lot of work, but it was work that provided for her family. With Ty, it was more than fun, and she was disappointed that it was almost over.

She plopped a bag on top of an already full dishpan of bagged corn. "Do you mind running this down to the freezer?" she asked Ty, who was chewing while cutting corn off the ears.

"Sure." He set his knife down and threw the cob in the bucket. "I think I should get paid for acting as your packhorse, though." His eyes glinted, and she didn't have much problem figuring out what, exactly, he thought he should get.

"We'll feed you lunch," she said primly. Kissing Ty would be more fun than doing corn, that was for sure. But she'd made that mistake once before. She arched her back to take the cramp out of it before putting her empty pan in the dishwater.

He shared a look with Gram, who was firmly on his side, after working under his flashing dimple and easy smile all morning.

"You keep working on her, and eventually you'll wear her down." Gram chortled. Louise did a double take. Seriously? This was Gram?

Normally Gram was more likely to be full of warnings and exhortations to be chaste.

Ty winked at Louise, like he knew exactly what she was thinking, before he opened the cellar door and went down.

Palmer and Ames took the husks out for the cattle, while Ty and she cleaned up the kitchen. They all ate a simple lunch of corn and turkey sandwiches with garden-ripe tomatoes and onions. Palmer and Ames sat at the ends of the table, while Gram and Pap sat on one side and Ty and Louise on the other.

Ty's large body threw heat, and his strong arms flexed as he ate. It was impossible not to be aware of him.

They took care of the few dishes, then Palmer and Ames went out to do more work at the barn and fields, and Gram and Pap went in to take a rest.

Louise finished wiping the table while Ty stood with a shoulder leaning against the fridge, watching her with one hand in his pocket, like he had nothing else better in the world to do.

"You want to work on Harvest Fest stuff in here or out on the porch?"

"I want to go to the porch, and we're not working until I rub your back some."

It ached. It always did after cutting corn all morning, and no one had ever offered to rub it. She should decline. She knew she should.

"Okay. I'll work, you rub."

"No." He pushed off the fridge. "I rub, you enjoy." His eyes flashed, and a curl of excitement went through her. Maybe a little uncertainty with it. This confident man in front of her was a lot different than the cocky but unsure boy he'd been.

"I don't know. I can get started—"

He took a step, and he was standing in front of her. One hand gripped the counter on either side of her. "You're going to take a ten-minute break. You're going to sit on that porch step, and you're going to close your eyes and relax while I take care of you. Ten minutes."

She blinked.

Maybe the uncertainty showed in her eyes because he added, "I'm touching only your back. And when you try to rip my shirt off, I'll fight you off." He grinned.

She returned it. "Okay. As long as you're fighting me off, let's do it." She pushed through, and just like she thought, he let her go, dropping his hand, so it only brushed her as she passed.

Pushing the screen door open, she walked out and sat on the second porch step. His body dropped down behind her, his legs strong and hard on either side. She leaned forward a little, wondering what he was going to do.

But he kept his word. It wasn't a sensual message. In fact, his fingers were almost impersonal.

"Tell me about Tella," he said.

Her favorite subject. And finally, she got to talk about her with her father. "She was seven pounds five ounces, and she was born on my graduation night." Louise closed her eyes as his fingers worked magic on her tired back.

He sucked in a breath. "You were valedictorian."

"Yes. I had a speech written that I never gave."

"Frig."

She chuckled. The years had softened that blow. "Tella was worth it. She's serious. Very much like a little adult, but she's the only child here on the ranch, so she imitates the people she's with, like every child does."

"Yeah."

"She loves hockey, and you're her favorite player. I have nothing to do with that, by the way. Palmer loves you too. Maybe that's what she picked up on, but your jersey was a Christmas gift, and she hasn't taken it off except to wash it since she got it."

His fingers stilled for a second before they started back up. "I noticed it looked worn." He blew a breath out. "That gives me the worst feeling inside. I know how expensive those jerseys are in the store, and I know that was something your family probably saved to get. I can get as many as I want. I give those things away. Yet, my own daughter..." He made a noise that sounded like a growl.

"We can't change the past. It's over. We can only learn from it and move forward."

"I know. But if I could change anything, what happened with you would be on the top of my list."

Did he mean what they'd done that last night? Or him leaving?

He continued, answering her unspoken question. "How I treated you and how I allowed my guilt to keep me from doing right by you. None of it was your fault, and yet, you're the one that suffered. I want to make that up to you."

"I don't want you with me just because you feel guilty or that you owe me."

"I'm with you because I enjoy being with you. I could assuage my guilt with money."

She let it go, feeling relaxed and loose as his fingers continued to knead her muscles with just the right amount of pressure.

"Tella does well in school, but she loves being on the ranch. She loves going to Sawyer's because he has a ton of things to do and she really feels like she's a help there. He doesn't have a house, though, so he can't really have her over when it gets cold."

"He doesn't have a house?"

"He just bought the place last fall. You'll have to see it. It needs a lot of work, but it was the right price, and things are crowded here."

She thought she did a good job of keeping any inflection out of her voice, but he caught on. "Palmer and Ames? You feel like you're in the way?"

"Not because of anything they do."

"Just because they need their own place."

"Yes."

"Hmm." There were a few beats of silence. "When does Tella get home from school?"

"Usually around four."

"Can I have her tomorrow after school?"

Fear swirled in her stomach, but she ignored it. Ty deserved to know his daughter. "Yes. I'll tell her about you tonight." She'd put it off too long. "I'm almost certain it will make her very happy."

"Can I have you tomorrow, too?"

She never took off work, and never with such short notice, but Patty would understand, and after all these years, the desire to do something as a family won out. "Yes."

Chapter 17

Sawyer had been in town and picked up Tella from school. When he dropped her off at the diner, he pulled Louise aside. Normally he just waved and maybe said a quick "hi," so she knew something was up.

Tella ran into the kitchen, where Louise had a sandwich and some veggies on a plate for her.

Sawyer waited until she disappeared. "Just wanted to make sure everything was okay."

"Yeah, why wouldn't it be?"

"I left last week because you told me to, not because I wanted to, and I'm still more than willing to give that guy a pounding. Just say the word, sister." Sawyer's jaw was set, and he looked like he'd go storming out if she but said to.

"No. Please." She put a hand on his arm. It was hard under her hand. He'd been doing a lot of work to try to get his ranch fixed up and still make enough on the few cattle he had to pay the mortgage. She wasn't sure how he was doing it. "There's more to it than what you know. I didn't even know everything. But trust me, it wasn't all him."

"I trust you. It's just that I've hated that guy, I didn't know who it was, but I hated him for a long time." Sawyer's eyes were still narrowed, and his jaw squarely locked.

"Palmer said basically the same thing. I didn't know you guys felt that way at all."

"How else could we feel? We know what kind of person you are. It's who you've always been. It wasn't hard to figure out that it was some sweet-talking pansy who left rather than do the right thing."

"That's not the way it was, I promise."

Sawyer was Norwegian through and through, and he didn't hug her, but he did put a hand on her shoulder, which was the equivalent to a massive hug in another culture. "Tella had a bunch of questions, and I deflected them all to you."

At Tella's age, she was still easily distracted, and she hadn't pushed Louise, with all the other things that were going on at the ranch. "I'm going on break right now, and I'm talking to her immediately." She'd put it off long enough.

He glanced around the diner where the supper crowd was just coming in. "You need me to cover for you for a few minutes in case it takes a little longer than you think?"

Lines of fatigue etched his face. Permanent since he'd bought his spread. She hated to add to his load. But she would appreciate not feeling the pressure to get right back to work. "Are you sure you don't mind?"

"Not at all. Give me your apron."

She grinned, knowing Sawyer would look just as manly wearing an apron as he would in the jeans and boots and button-down he had on. "You probably ought to take your hat off."

He grabbed it from his head. "Throw it behind the counter."

His hair had a definite band from wearing the hat. She grinned.

He grinned back, the dimples in his cheeks popping, even with the stubble on his face.

Louise peered through the window across the street at the gym. Normally Ty had been going to the gym and coming in afterward. Sawyer would be true to his word and wouldn't start a fight, but it might be wise to get back out fast anyway.

She took a breath, seeing Tella sitting at the counter in the back of the kitchen, munching on her sandwich, and watching Sawyer and her talk.

Louise tried to calm the rearing horses in her stomach. It was hard to do anything that might hurt the bond she had with Tella.

"Hey, honey," she said, pulling out a stool and sitting down beside her daughter. They were far enough away from Rebel and Jackson that she wasn't afraid they'd overhear. Plus, they were busy with the supper orders.

"Hey, Mom."

"Did you have a good day at school?"

"Yep. I like it when Uncle Sawyer picks me up. Everyone thinks his truck is cool. We should go live with him. Now that Uncle Palmer has Ames, Uncle Sawyer needs us more." She took a casual bite of her sandwich and chewed.

Maybe Tella was feeling the pinch of being crowded in their house, too. Louise filed that thought away. "Sawyer doesn't have a house."

"He lived there all last winter, and he was fine. We can do it too, Mom. And I'm a big help to him. He said so."

"I'm sure you are. But you'll be in school this winter."

"You could homeschool me."

"When I'm not waitressing and editing?"

"Sure. I'm easy. I do all my work without complaining, and I learn fast." She took a bite of her sandwich in the unconcerned air children had.

"I don't think I can."

She swallowed. Her trusting eyes met Louise's. "Sawyer said you were the smartest kid in your class."

"Maybe not the smartest, but I worked the hardest."

Tella nodded like that made sense to her, and maybe it did. Louise had always tried to emphasize the value of hard work.

"I need to talk to you about something else."

"Ty Hanson?" Tella asked immediately.

"Yes."

"I tried to ask Uncle Sawyer what was going on, but he just gave me the runaround, so I gave up. And I keep forgetting when we're home."

Her little shoulder lifted in a shrug, and she took another bite of her sandwich.

"Well, uh..." This was the thing that Louise had dreaded all her life. "Let me tell you what I have to say, and if you have any questions, you can ask them, okay?"

"Sure."

"So, you've asked about your dad, and I've always said he left and didn't come back."

"What does my dad have to do with this?"

Louise raised her brows.

"Oh. Sorry." Tella stuck her sandwich in her mouth.

Louise smiled before she sobered. "You know Ty Hanson went to school with us."

"Yeah."

"Please don't talk with your mouth full." She tried not to let her voice hold the snap that it wanted to.

"Sorry."

"I knew Ty, too. He... He had to..." Louise didn't know how to say it, other than come right out. "He's your father."

Tella's eyes got big.

"He did leave, but he had to because of college and hockey. And he didn't call, but his dad died, and he was hurt and confused for a long time."

"Is he still hurt and confused?" Tella asked hesitantly.

"No."

"So he wants to be my dad now?" Hope blossomed in her eyes.

"Yes."

"He's going to come live with us, too?" Tella bounced on her seat, her sandwich forgotten in her hand.

"No."

She deflated. "Why not?"

"We're not married."

"But you could be. It isn't hard to get married, is it?" The eager expression on her face hit Louise in her chest.

"No, but that's a big commitment."

"You're good for it, Mom!"

Louise's mouth hung open.

Tella pumped a fist. "My dad is a hockey superstar? Are you sure, Mom?"

"Yes."

"Oh my goodness, I can't believe it. I can't believe it! Like, seriously, wow!" Tella bounced in her seat.

"So, you're okay with this?"

"Mom? Are you kidding? I have the coolest dad ever!" Her eyes fell. "Are you sure he wants me? I mean, where has he been?"

"How about you ask me?" Ty stood in the doorway, a question on his face, with his gaze directed at Louise.

Louise nodded. "I need to get back to work. If you need me for anything, Tella, you know you can come get me."

"I know." Her eyes were glued on Ty in something that looked a lot like hero worship. Louise hoped Ty was up to this. She stood and met Ty's gaze before leaving the kitchen.

TY LOOKED AT HIS DAUGHTER. His *daughter*. She looked so much like Louise. But he could see himself in her too. His heart stirred and tightened, and the protection instinct rose up in him strong and hard. He battled it back. He couldn't come on too strong. He needed to take his time and earn her trust.

"Hi," he said, thinking he sounded lame. What did one say to one's daughter who had spent the first eight years of her life not even knowing who he was, while he didn't even know that she existed?

"Hi," she said back. "I'm Tella. And Mom said that you're my dad."

He sat down on the stool that Louise had just been on. "I am."

"She said you wanted me now. But I'm not sure, because you don't live with me. Why not?"

Ty grunted. That was an easy question. "Because I'm stupid."

Tella wasn't expecting that answer by the surprise that crossed her face.

He put his elbows on his knees and looked straight into Tella's eyes. "I'm sorry. I'm really sorry, Tella, that I wasn't here."

"Mom said your dad died and you were hurt and confused or something."

He nodded, trying not to twist his hands together. "Yeah."

"That didn't seem to stop you from playing hockey." Tella's eyes narrowed, and she sounded more like an adult than a school-aged kid.

"My dad coached me in hockey. It was the one thing I knew I could do that would have made him proud if he were here."

"Oh." Her eyes fell.

"He would have been proud of you, too."

She looked up. "Really?"

"Yep, and my mom is going to be over the moon with excitement and happiness."

"Your mom is Miss Donna, right?"

"Yep, and that makes Miss Donna your grandmother."

Wonder crept across the little girl's face. "I have a grandmother."

Ty made a note to ask Louise about her parents. If he remembered correctly, they'd basically dumped their kids off on their parents here in Sweet Water and left. He thought he'd heard they were at Palmer's wedding, but he wouldn't have recognized them. Hadn't heard anything about them since.

"You do. And she already loves you very much. She's going to be ecstatic when she learns you're her granddaughter."

Tella tilted her head. "Can I tell people that you're my dad?"

"Sure." He would love it. He wanted to finally stand with Louise, and he was proud of Tella.

"How much am I going to see you?"

"As much as I can."

"All the time? You'll live with us? You'll marry Mom?"

"I want to."

Tella's eyes grew wide. "Really? Does Mom know?"

"I don't know. I made some promises to your mom that I didn't keep, and she needs to learn to trust me again. It's going to take some time."

"Maybe I could go to one of your games?" Tella asked, hope shining in her eyes.

Ty would have given her anything at that moment. "I'd love that. You can bring your mom."

"She doesn't like the fights." Tella gave him a conspiratorial look. "They're my favorite part."

Ty laughed. "I'm not in that many fights."

"I know," Tella said. "You play good hockey. That's what Uncle Palmer said."

"That's a compliment. Thanks." He cleared his throat. "Your mom said it was okay if you spent the day with me tomorrow. What do you think?"

Her eyes got big. "Really?"

His mouth kicked up. "Yeah. Maybe we'll let your mom come too. See if I can try to charm her a little."

"Yes!"

He and Tella talked for over an hour. Mostly with her pelting him with questions. He didn't mind. He loved that Tella seemed to accept him with such ease.

Time flew by. She came out and sat with him and read a book while he ate. Louise kept glancing at them, a mixture of hope and happiness on her face that stirred his heart and made him want to be more, be better, for her.

Once he was done eating, he figured if Sawyer could bus tables, he could do it too. So he told Tella that he was going to help her mom, then got up and started cleaning tables off for her. He hated to see her work so hard, but if he bussed the tables, she'd have more time for her editing, which was sitting on the back counter.

Ty couldn't have been happier as he helped Louise and Tella into their car after they left the diner for the night. He didn't say anything more than, "I'll follow you home and see you in the morning."

Things went better than he'd expected with Tella, and that was a major step in getting Louise to trust him. Not that he wanted to use Tella to get to Louise, but he could prove that he was sincere by the way he treated their daughter.

His phone rang on the way home. The screen said it was Georgia. He answered on the hands-free.

"What's up, kiddo?"

"I'm a full-grown woman."

"You're a half-grown woman."

"Shut up," she said irritably.

"That's not nice," he chided.

"It's not nice to call me a kid."

"You look like a kid."

"I do not."

"Did you want something? Or did you just call to argue?" Ty's good humor kept the smile on his face. He really needed to stop teasing his sister, but that's what brothers were for.

"How'd it go?"

"Perfect. Tella loves me and is happy I'm her dad."

"That's great."

"Yep. But you know, I think I've been pushing too hard with Louise."

"Maybe."

"I know exactly what I want, and I've been angling to get it. I think I need to back off. Take it slow. It's just going to take time for her to see that I'm not disappearing again. So, I'll just take this next year and court her, kind of, I guess. Maybe pop the question next fall. We'll have a nice, long engagement. Maybe a year. And a huge wedding with all the bells and whistles. A huge church, the beautiful dress, the decorations, and great food at the reception. I think in two years that could be my reality." It would be hard as anything to wait that long for Louise, but he wanted her to have plenty of time to see that he wasn't going anywhere.

"Uh. No."

"What?" He thought Georgia would be all on board with that. Everyone said he was only after one thing the last time and left when he got it. He and Louise would prove them all wrong. He'd be nothing but a gentleman. He wouldn't even kiss her until at least next summer. Which would be torture, but he could do it. Louise was worth it.

"That's too long. Um..." Georgia seemed to be struggling, and it finally dawned on Ty that he might be missing something.

"What?"

"I...I can't say. Just please don't wait that long."

"I thought you'd tell me my plan was perfect."

"It is, in a normal situation. But..."

"Just spit it out," he said in frustration. She wasn't making any sense.

"Just, please trust me. It needs to be before Christmas." Georgia sounded completely confident.

But that shattered everything he'd been thinking. Louise would never trust him again that fast. "How am I going to do that?"

"Try. Please."

"Okay."

They hung up, and Ty drove the rest of the way home wondering what in the world Georgia could possibly know that he didn't, that made it necessary for Louise to get married by Christmas. No matter. He trusted Georgia on a lot of things, but he knew he was right with Louise. She needed him to take it slow.

His mom was just pulling in when he got home. He hurried out to help her unload her car.

"Just leave everything on the porch. I'll sort it out tomorrow," his mom said as they each carried armfuls of things in.

"Okay. I have something to tell you if you're not too tired." He set her stuff down and started back for the last load.

"Never too tired for my children."

"I think it's good news," he called over his shoulder.

She was sitting at the table, a bottle of water and a plate of grapes in front of her, when he walked in. He pulled a chair out and sat down, his arms resting on the table, his hands clasped.

"Good trip?"

"Yes. Profitable. Which is the best kind."

He shared a smile with her.

"What's your news?" she asked.

"Tella is my daughter."

There was not a hint of surprise on his mother's face. Her smile was serene.

"You knew," he accused, his brows raised.

"Your dad told me about your argument. I knew you'd been meeting her, and if you weren't in love with her, you were close." She fingered her drink. "He and I disagreed on the right way to handle it. I'm afraid I argued with him, even more forcefully than you did." Regret clouded her features. "I was yelling at him that it should be your choice what you wanted to do with your life, when he clutched his chest." His mother's hand shook as she rolled a grape around. "It took me a long time to get over that guilt. I had no right to speak to him so. We never argued. But Louise was a wonderful girl, and you had a solid head on your shoulders. I was sure you'd make good decisions if we just backed off." She shook her head sadly. "I wasn't entirely correct, now, was I?"

"It was only that last night, Mom, I swear it. I'd treated her with the utmost respect until then. But fighting with Dad on top of leaving for school...I shouldn't have gone alone, because I couldn't stop..." If only he could do it over. He'd do that night so much differently.

"It's okay. It's done now. But I was almost sure when I found out she was expecting that the baby was yours. But you never showed up to complete the picture."

"She never told me, and you never said." He couldn't help being burned about that.

"It wasn't my place. If you would have ever asked about her, I would have told you whatever you wanted to know. But you didn't." She popped a grape into her mouth.

He let out a frustrated breath. "I would have come home. I would have married her."

"Maybe that's why she never told you."

"I'm sure it is." He closed his eyes. It was done and over. He just had to try to atone. "Tella knows that you're her gram. She loves you."

"I could always see you in her. What are you going to do now?"

"I'm trying to court Louise." He ran a hand over his head. "I have a couple of weeks until I need to get back for hockey. Not much time."

"I think Louise has always been in love with you."

He studied his mother. "You think?"

Her face glowed. "Yes. It might be easier than you think. Especially with Tella. I know she wants a home and a family for that little girl."

"Me too."

His mother reached over and patted his hand. "You can do it, son."

"I'd like to buy the ranch," he said, in an abrupt subject change.

His mother's smile grew larger. "I was hoping you would."

Chapter 18

Ty picked Louise up and drove into town to get Tella from school. He held an umbrella over them as they walked to his car. Of all days, it had to choose the evening he was finally spending with Louise to be overcast and rainy. It was the forecast for the entire night.

However, he'd never let a little thing like rain stand in his way.

Louise looked amazing in jeans and a sweater. "I wasn't sure what to wear," she said as she held the door for Tella.

"That's perfect." He lowered his voice. "You look good."

Her lips tilted as she slid into his car. He noted Tella was wearing his jersey, which made his soul feel satisfied deep inside.

He'd barely started out of the drive when Tella said, "Where are we going?"

He shot a look at Louise. Her face held curiosity, too. "I'd been planning on saddling the horses and taking you two out for a ride and a picnic." He looked out at the low sky. "But I thought maybe that wouldn't be such an enjoyable thing with the rain."

"That would be fun!" Tella called from the back. "I love riding horses."

Louise tilted her head. "At least it's not cold."

"True." Although the colder rains of autumn were coming. Soon. "But I have resources and friends in convenient places, and—" He paused, drawing the suspense out.

"What? What?" Tella called from the back seat.

"We're still going to have a picnic. We're just going to have it in the barn. I borrowed a projector, set up a screen, and thought we'd have a movie too. I also brought some games out." He'd had to dig those up out of the closet, but he thought Tella would enjoy them. It'd taken some work to get the barn ready. The people who were renting the fields kept some equipment on the barn floor, but there were still some square bales in the loft. He'd hung up an old sheet for the "screen," and he'd brought out several blankets so Louise wouldn't have to sit on prickly hay. Not that he figured she'd care.

He'd never be able to get away with a date like this with any of the girls he'd dated in the city. But he thought this was something Louise would enjoy.

"Yay!" Tella shouted.

And Tella.

"You have a projector?" Louise asked, disbelief lacing her voice.

"We don't own it. My mom just happens to be the one who keeps the church's projector. She gave me permission to use it." He gave her a sideways glance. "After all, it's not like I'm a freeloader at church. I'm co-chairing the Harvest Fest committee."

Louise snorted, as he'd intended. She was going to be laughing by the end of the day if he had anything to do with it.

LOUISE AND TELLA LAUGHED as Ty finished telling the story about his dad and the hog that got away. He figured any story that ended with him covered in mud from head to toe and a hog headed toward town would tickle their funny bones. It had.

"Did you ever catch it?" Tella asked, after she was done laughing.

"Nope. It's probably still out there somewhere."

Her dark blue eyes got big. "Do you think?"

He was stretched out on his side, his belly full, his heart happy, his head resting on his hand. "Every time I hear about someone shooting a feral pig in Florida or Texas, I wonder if that old sow didn't think it was time to migrate to a warmer climate and live out her days where she didn't have to worry about surviving the winter."

Tella's face scrunched up. She imitated his position on the opposite side of the blanket, facing him. Louise hadn't relaxed quite that much and sat primly on the end between their feet. Which was fine. He had a great view of her, and he hadn't supposed she would lie down beside him so he could tuck her into his stomach, wrap his arm around her, and bury his nose in her hair.

"I don't know why it would want to leave North Dakota. There's no snow in Florida, and Uncle Palmer says North Dakota is the best place in the world to live."

Ty caught Louise's small smile at that, and his insides shivered. He wouldn't be able to settle down in North Dakota for years. Not until his hockey career was over, and he planned on playing as long as he could.

Although he loved being back on the farm. The memories were here but not as painful as he'd feared. Coming back had resurrected his ranching dreams, which was always what he'd planned on doing until hockey had presented the opportunities it had.

"Honey, Ty's been a lot more places than Uncle Palmer has. Maybe he thinks there's somewhere better."

Tella's face drew down like thunderclouds lowering over the prairie.

"There's a lot of pretty places in the world," he said, not wanting to lie. But he supposed it was the same as there being a lot of pretty women in the world. "But there's just one place that's home." And there was just one girl that was perfect for him. All the other girls he'd dated over the years were missing something. Sometimes they were missing a lot of things. But he'd never had that feeling with Louise. Not in high school, not now.

She studied his face, and he wished he knew what she was thinking. Wished he could sit up, pull her into himself, and talk about how she was everything he wanted, but she needed time. He intended to give it to her.

"Ready for the movie?" They'd played every game he'd brought out, and the remains of their picnic lay on the blanket in front of them. The light was fading, and it was getting cooler.

"Yes!" Tella called out.

He watched Louise nod.

"I'll get it ready." He sat up then pushed to a standing position, his leg giving one small twitch but nothing major. He had an appointment next week at the doctor's two hours away, but he could feel that he was healing. He'd be in shape for the season, easy. His trainer was pushing to ramp up his workouts, and his PT was giving the green light.

Only, somehow, the excitement of starting the season was tempered for the first time by the idea that maybe there was somewhere else he'd rather be.

It took him a few minutes to get the movie going with the projector hooked up to his laptop. By then, Louise had the blanket cleaned off. Tella lay on her stomach, with her head in her hands, facing the screen. Louise had moved from the end of the blanket and sat crossed-legged behind Tella at her feet.

Taking chances was part of his job, and he barely debated before he sat down behind Louise and a little to the side, so that Tella's feet were in front of him on his right and Louise was in front of him on his left.

"This okay?" he asked low to Louise as the music from the movie began, loud and cheerful.

"You're going to watch the movie over my shoulder?"

"It's a nice shoulder."

Her air puffed out in a stifled laugh. "Not better than the movie."

"It is, actually. But I can see the screen just fine if that's what you're worried about."

She took a breath. "No. You're just...close, that's all."

"It bother you?" he asked, not sure if that was a good thing or a bad thing.

"No," she breathed out.

His heart spun.

Part of playing good hockey was knowing when to press your advantage. "So I could move closer?"

The movie began with action, and he was afraid it might have drowned out his request. But he didn't want to draw Tella's attention to the fact that he was trying to snuggle with her mother.

A little fear or uncertainty flashed across Louise's face. He hated it, and he hated himself for causing it. "I'm not leaving you again," he said, his voice full of sand and gravel because of the guilt in his heart. He couldn't expect her to believe it just because he said so, but he had to do something to erase that look from her face.

She closed her eyes before turning her head back toward the screen.

It wasn't a yes, but it wasn't a no, either. He slid up a little. "You'll be more comfortable if you lean against me." He forced the next words out of his closed-up throat. "I promise I won't touch you with my hands."

Her head twisted back, and her eyes narrowed as though gauging the truth in his promise. "I kept it the last time."

She lifted her chin just slightly. He kept eye contact as he slid forward, putting one leg on either side of her.

Heat flushed in her cheeks, and her breathing became less steady. It matched his.

Why did he make those stupid promises? Because he wanted to brush her flyaway hair away from her face and tuck it behind her ear, then run his fingers through it, pulling her toward him, kissing her until they were both breathless, which would take about two seconds on his part, anyway.

"Someday I want to see your hair down." He hadn't planned on those words coming out.

He hadn't realized his chest could get any tighter as she reached up and pulled her hair out of its holder. She fluffed it with her fingers, holding his eyes. His lids were heavy, and he had trouble holding them open. They drooped as his fingers tingled. But he didn't move. Barely breathed.

There was a vulnerability on her face that pulled at his heart. He wanted her trust. It wasn't going to be an easy thing to earn.

She dropped her hands and turned back toward the movie. Slowly her body eased back into his. His hands balled where they held his weight behind him on the hay. He wanted to wrap his arms around her and pull her back into him, but he'd promised not to touch her, and she was trusting him.

So he took what he could get. The fresh-air scent of her hair. The press of her back against his stomach. The heat of her slim body through his t-shirt. Her trust that he would keep his word.

If only the movie would last forever, but it ended, and Louise leaned up.

Tella sat up, twisting around. "I have to use the restroom."

"You can go in the house. Miss Donna is there."

"Brush yourself off," Louise said. "And you can probably call her 'grandma' if you want to."

"Really?" Tella asked with bright eyes.

"Ask her," Louise replied.

Ty should have thought of that earlier, but they'd come and gone straight to the barn, so they'd not seen his mother.

"We're going to pack this stuff up and come in shortly," he said to Tella, stuffing down his disappointment as Louise moved completely away from him, brushing some hay off the blanket.

"Okay," Tella said as she threw a leg around the ladder and climbed the short distance to the ground. She skipped away, slipping out the wooden door and closing it behind her.

Louise didn't stand, but she moved around, stacking the games and putting the food basket aside.

She talked as she worked, keeping her head down and not meeting his eyes. "Thanks so much for having us this evening. Tella really enjoyed herself, and I appreciate you spending some time with her. Even if you don't plan on seeing her much—"

She stopped abruptly as he took hold of her arm. When he'd asked her to lean against him, he'd promised not to touch her. But that was over.

Her surprised eyes shot to his face. "Break up with Paul." He hated the begging that was in his voice. "Please."

Her eyes searched his, wide and uncertain.

"Don't go out with anyone else," he continued in the same tone. "Just me." He didn't need to push her for a commitment. She could take her time learning to trust him again. He could take years before he asked her to share his life, which was what he really wanted. But he needed this one thing. He needed her loyalty.

"I broke up with him that night after the movie," she said softly.

Heat from her arm warmed his hand. Relief soothed his heart. "Thank you."

"It doesn't have anything to do with you. I thought it would work, but it was just another mistake..." Her voice trailed off.

He flinched.

She shook her head. "It's over with him. It should never have started. I thought I was doing a good thing for Tella, but it wouldn't have been."

She looked a little more disappointed than the situation called for, in his opinion, and she'd made sure he knew he wasn't the reason she'd broken up with Paul.

He leaned forward, unable to keep his fingertips from running along her hairline and down the angle of her jaw. Her blue eyes darkened. He did affect her. In some way.

"I know you don't have any reason to believe me," he whispered, inches from her face. "But I know what's out there doesn't compare to what's right here." He moved his fingers along her cheek. Maybe he wasn't clear. "No one else compares to you."

She turned her head and shook it a little. "I've seen the pictures, Ty. You've been with a hundred other women who are a lot more beautiful than me."

Tension in her shoulders spoke of the hurt those pictures had caused, and he cursed his stupidity. How difficult it must have been for her to be here, raising his child, seeing him with other women.

He knew what everyone thought, and he'd never made a single effort to keep them from thinking any differently. It would sound like lies now, but he had to say, "None of them meant anything to me. To me, you're the most beautiful woman in the world."

Her lip pulled back. As he suspected, she didn't really believe him. What could he do to convince her to trust him?

Kissing her probably wasn't the answer, but that's what he seemed bent on doing as his body leaned even farther toward her. She lifted her head and didn't back away. It gave him hope and caused his heart to thump, heavy and fast.

But he stopped. Everyone had said he had only been after one thing. He wasn't going to kiss her. Not yet. As much as he wanted to. He put his lips on her forehead instead. Even that caused his heart to shake.

She didn't pull away, and he kept his lips against her skin. "I want to kiss you. My whole body aches for it. But I want your trust more than I want anything else." He skimmed his lips along her forehead, feeling the soft skin. It wasn't enough, but he couldn't have more. Not now.

He pulled back, hating that she had to work because of him and hating that he had to take her home now.

She nodded and they stood, gathering up the picnic things and heading toward the house.

Chapter 19

That week, Ty seemed to be around as much as he could be. He helped with canning and with Pap. He helped Palmer build a ramp for their porch. He went with Louise to Gram's appointment in a bigger town an hour away. He bought her and Gram a nice dinner in a much fancier restaurant than they were used to.

He helped at the diner, bussing tables and even serving some food, if Louise was busy with editing. He and Louise talked about Harvest Fest and made plans for it. One week slipped into two.

By the third week, he still hadn't kissed her. Although they were bantering like old friends now, and she felt more comfortable with him than she ever had with anyone before, she didn't want to be the friend he hung out with until hockey started and he left for good. The day of his departure was the day after Harvest Fest, but she did not allow herself to dwell on that.

She didn't have time to think about it the morning of Harvest Fest.

The day dawned clear but chilly. Normal mid-September weather for North Dakota. Ty had wanted to pick her up and take her in when he'd dropped her off last night, but she wanted to have her car, just in case she needed to run home.

He was waiting at the park when she pulled in at daylight, unloading boxes from his truck. They'd done some decorating the night before, but because of wind and the off chance it would rain, they waited until today to put the majority of things up.

Ty came over and opened her door.

"You already have the tables set up. That's great!"

He grinned. "I didn't need light to set up tables." One of his big shoulders moved up. "Well, nothing more than my car headlights."

She shook her head. "You do know this isn't like a normal thing, where if you do a good job, you get promoted to an easier job?"

He tilted his head.

She continued. "It's more like if you do a good job, you get punished by everyone saying you did a great job and you should do it again next year. Plus, they'll volunteer you for something else, too, just to make sure you don't get too proud of yourself for pulling it off."

"As long as you're my co-chair, I'm game."

She laughed and hit his shoulder lightly. "You've been the brawn *and* the brains." Which was true. He'd done a lot of planning at the restaurant while she worked. He'd ask questions then write down ideas. He'd even bought Mrs. Aucker dinner, at least four or five times, as he ran his ideas by her. In Louise's opinion, that was very brave of him.

"But I like working with you." His eyes glinted down at her, and she paused in pulling out the tablecloths, looking over her shoulder at him. "I'm going to kiss you today," he said, as casually as he might have said the wind was blowing.

Her eyes widened, and her heart stuttered and gasped as his grin turned wolfish. "Just warning you."

How was she supposed to work all day with *that* in the back of her head? "How about you just do it now and get it over with?"

His booming laugh filled the early morning air.

"That's romantic." He stepped closer, his hand going to her waist. "If you don't want me kissing you, you'd better say so, because it's going to hurt my feelings if my lips are on yours and I'm going crazy and you're just standing there wishing I'd get it over with."

His hand on her waist did funny things to her heart and mind. Made one go faster and one slower. She had never flirted, but dang, if her eyes didn't bat and she didn't give him a sassy smile. "I don't know, Ty. You might have lost your touch since high school."

He growled, half-pretend, half-real-sounding, and put his other hand on her waist, drawing her closer. And closer. Her chest touched his, and he leaned down. "If I haven't gotten better since high school, you're going to work with me and let me practice until kissing me is your favorite pastime. Until you can't think when I kiss you. Until all you can say after I'm done kissing you is 'yes, Ty,' 'more, Ty,' 'please more, Ty.'" His wolfish grin was back. She felt like she was almost at that point now, and all he had done was put his hands on her waist.

Well, she didn't want to be the only one whose brain had flown south for the winter. Dropping the tablecloths, she ran her hands up his chest and out his shoulders, following the curves to caress his biceps before moving up and around the back of his neck. She pressed closer while playing with the short hair at the base of his skull. "Yes, Ty," she whispered with a twinkle in her eye. "More, Ty," she breathed softly as his eyes drooped and his hands tightened on her waist. "Please more, Ty," she said in a throaty, husky sound that she didn't even recognize as her own.

He groaned and laughed at the same time, dropping his head to her ear. "Okay, okay, you've made your point. You drive me insane. I can't stop thinking about you, and when I finally do kiss you, I know my brain is going to disappear. Have mercy on me, lady. The town already thinks it was me that took advantage of you. They don't know all you have to do is whisper my name and I'll do whatever you want." His breath brushed by her ear, making electric sparks fly through her body, while his words touched her wounded spirit, deep inside.

He lifted his head slightly, his eyes still half-closed. She touched her tongue to her top lip, then her bottom, and smiled a smile as old as Eve. "Ty," she whispered.

He groaned, and this time, there was no laughter in it. "Stop," he breathed out, but it sounded more like a plea to continue. He shook his head and dropped his arms to his sides, but didn't move out from under her hands. "I'm not doing that to you again."

"Maybe I want you to kiss me." She did. She wanted him to. Right now, in the park where God and everyone could see.

"No. Not now. Not here." He finally stepped back, slowly, like it cost a great effort. "It's only been four weeks. You need to know. Everyone needs to know that I'm serious. I'm not hiding this, I'm not leaving you. That you're more than just a physical relationship to me. They're not going to wonder who your boyfriend is and whether he's coming back." His voice got deep and rough. "They're not going to wonder who the father of your children is because I'm going to be there holding them. We'll raise them together and make our living together. I'm *going* to be with you."

"Hey, you two. This park isn't going to decorate itself." Mrs. Aucker came stumping over, her tremendous girth in no way slowing her down.

Ty's eyes didn't move from Louise's. Her whole body felt trembly and weak, while her heart fluttered and bounced in her chest. Whatever his desired outcome of that little speech, he'd managed to make her want to kiss him about a thousand times more than she had to begin with. But she drew a shaky breath and tore her eyes away from his.

He waited a good five seconds before he stepped back and bent to pick up her tablecloths. Mrs. Aucker had reached them by the time he handed them to Louise.

"Ty, you did this girl wrong. Everyone in town knows it. But everyone also knows she's got you wrapped around her little finger." She huffed then rolled her eyes. "Louise, tell this boy to stop mooning after you. We've got a festival that's starting in two hours, and you might have been up at the crack of dawn, but you don't have anything more done here this morning than you did last night."

The festival went well, not that Louise noticed, but everyone said so. She walked around in a haze most of the day. They had cleaned up, Ty had followed her and Tella home, and she was just drifting off to sleep with a smile on her face when she realized that Ty never did kiss her that day.

LOUISE WALKED INTO church with Tella the next morning. From the smiles of her fellow worshippers and the hearty congratulations she received, she could safely assume that Harvest Festival was a success. Although the true test would be when the church tallied the money it made to send to missions.

Still, she allowed herself to feel grateful to Ty. She couldn't take responsibility for half of what went on yesterday. He'd come up with so many ideas and improvements. Of course, he'd said that was because he'd been to festivals in other towns and gotten ideas there, but still, he'd done a great job, put in a lot of time and work, and he deserved more than half the credit.

Louise was at the piano when he walked in, so she really didn't get to hear what anyone said to him. She didn't have a great view of the congregation from her corner, but she was thrilled when Pastor Houpe announced that they'd made more money at Harvest Fest this year than they ever had before.

He thanked Ty and her, and they sang the last hymn before the sermon. She was halfway down to her seat before she realized that Ty was sitting in her seat. Right by where she'd left her purse and Bible.

This was a new development—he'd always sat with his mother before—and her step faltered, even as her eyes met his, confident and sure. He was raised in this small town, same as she, and he knew exactly what it would mean for her to sit with him in church. Like they were engaged.

Rumors had flown around for the last few weeks, as people started finding out who Tella's father was, and he'd borne the nasty glances and irritated looks and hateful comments. The ones that said he'd known she was pregnant and left anyway.

Louise had supposed it would help him to sit with her in church, and she'd almost suggested it herself a time or two.

Maybe that's why he waited. Because he wasn't going to take the easy way out of smoothing things over by giving her attention now.

No. He'd waited weeks for the gossip to die down before he moved to her seat.

Her heart clenched as she forced her feet to continue to move toward the big man with his arm casually draped over the back of the pew where her purse and Bible sat. His eyes tracked her movement down the steps of the platform and down the aisle, past Tella who sat with Donna. His mother beamed at her.

The pastor droned on in the background, giving the scripture references, and pages crinkled as people opened their Bibles. Louise barely heard it as she walked closer.

Ty's eyes danced as she arrived at her pew and slid in, sitting primly an arm's length from him, her purse and Bible between them.

He leaned over. "Everyone's going to think that you don't like me much." He sighed almost inaudibly. "If you want to stay there, it's fine, but you'd save me some teasing after church if you slide a little closer."

She twisted her head to look at him, seeing the cocky attitude. But this close, she could also see the shadow of insecurity that threaded across his features. It pricked at her heart.

Sure, she'd been the subject of gossip for years, far longer than the weeks he'd spent with tongues wagging behind his back at what a horrible person he was for leaving her, alone and pregnant. But she wouldn't deliberately wish that on anyone, and she really felt like if he wasn't justified, she at least understood why. She also knew he hadn't known about his child.

His eyes held hers. Her expression softened, and a spark of triumph came into his gaze before she slid closer, past where his hand lay on the back of his pew, and into the circle of his embrace. He picked up her Bible and purse and set them on his other side, then he slid closer, obliterating the six inches between them, still balancing his own Bible on his knee.

His lips feathered her ear. "Relax, Louise. Maybe once you get done looking like you're scared to death of me, you could act like you like me a little."

She whispered back, "I like you a lot, you big doofus. But you know as well as I do that if I sit beside you in church, especially this close—" she probably looked like she was a mouse poking out of his shirt pocket "—they'll have us married by next month."

He grinned, slow and devastating to her insides. A knowing grin that said he absolutely knew what she said was true and he was perfectly fine with it.

She allowed her lips to turn up and made her shoulders relax.

Pastor was halfway through the sermon when she realized that no one would have her married by next month, because Ty was leaving.

Chapter 20

The change in Louise was sudden and dramatic. One minute, she was snuggled under his arm, her warmth pressing against his side; the next, she had stiffened and pulled away. Just slightly, but enough that he noticed. He couldn't get her to look at him, and he hated to whisper as the pastor's sermon wound down.

He'd be asking her as soon as the service was over.

Except he didn't get to her. She was still playing the postlude when he was surrounded by people congratulating him on the success of Harvest Fest. The pastor mentioned Christmas festivals, but Ty declined immediately, since he'd be in the middle of hockey season.

"In fact, I leave this afternoon for training camp."

"Oh." The pastor's face fell. "Well, you'll be back after the season ends in April. You can help with tractor days, Easter, Memorial Day, summer solstice, and the Fourth of July. We'll need floats for at least nine parades and..." The pastor continued to speak. Ty was okay with any of that as long as Louise was beside him. If she wanted to help the church participate in every parade and festival the town did—and there were a lot of parades and festivals—he was game.

But he didn't say that to the pastor. He'd suddenly realized the piano music had stopped and Louise was no longer on the platform. But he couldn't see her anywhere. Waiting impatiently for the pastor to get to a place where Ty could interrupt him, Ty finally excused himself only to be stopped by well-meaning people who wanted to congratulate him on a good Harvest Fest, or wish him well on the upcoming season, or even ask about whether or not he was helping with more church festivals.

By the time he'd made it out to the pavilion, Louise was nowhere in sight. He did see Tella eating with his mom, so he ignored the rumbling in his stomach that said it was well past lunchtime and walked over to them.

"Hey," he said.

Tella jumped up and gave him a hug. He didn't deserve her adoration, but he hugged her back.

"Where's your plate? Aren't you eating with us?" she asked.

"I was going to, but I thought your mom would be out here."

"She didn't feel well and went home. Palmer and Ames said they would take Tella home with them. That just makes sense." His mother held a spoonful of mashed potatoes suspended in midair. "Is there a problem?"

"No. I was busy, and she didn't tell me."

His mother's look grew thoughtful. "You're leaving," she stated softly.

Could that really be it? But he'd tried so hard to let her know that he was with her no matter what. Even sitting with her in church today was designed to show her that he didn't care who all knew he was sweet on her. It was basically a way to announce to the town that she was his and they were together.

But none of that guaranteed that he would call. Or that he'd come back. Really, all those things he'd done would make it worse if he left and abandoned her again.

He hadn't told her how he felt. But all the talking in the world wouldn't guarantee that he'd come back. Only his actual return would do that. He had every good intention of calling, texting, and flying back home as much as he could, but he also knew how all-consuming playing a professional sport could be. Everyone wanted him, all the time.

Maybe she'd go with him.

Lights turned on in his brain. Why hadn't he asked her before this?

"I'm driving out." He glanced at Tella. "Just to be sure she's okay."

"I think that's a good idea," his mother said.

"But first, can I get a picture of you, Tella?" He had plenty on his phone, but he'd never have too many pictures of his daughter.

She smiled, and he snapped a couple of shots. Then he took several with her and his mother together, trying to savor the last time with his daughter for he didn't know how long but all the while feeling a driving need to go to Louise.

"Can I see?" Tella asked, holding out her hand for his phone.

He handed it to her. "Can you make sure I get it back? I should be leaving for the airport soon, but I need to see your mom first."

"Yes. I will," his mother promised.

He hugged Tella tight, wishing once again that Louise would move to Pittsburgh with him. He hated leaving his daughter, especially when he was just getting to know her.

Louise's car was parked at her house when he got there, but she didn't answer the door. It wasn't locked, so he pushed it open and called out, "Louise, are you in here?"

He didn't hear anything. She could be outside, but he had a feeling she wasn't. His need to see her was greater than his desire not to trespass, so he pushed the door the rest of the way open and stepped inside.

She wasn't in the kitchen. Nor the living room. He didn't check in the last room downstairs, knowing that was where her gram and pap stayed.

The stairs loomed large in front of him.

Remember what happened the last time before you left.

Oh, he knew. And he absolutely was not making that mistake again, but he needed to see her. Maybe his mother was wrong and she really was sick.

That thought was enough to prod him up the stairs, taking them three at a time, making enough noise so he wouldn't startle her, whatever she was doing.

He had no idea which room was hers. He stared at the four closed doors. Two were cracked.

Figuring the one at the end was a bathroom, he stretched so he could see in the other open door. A pink comforter with lots of stuffed animals covered the bed. Tella's room. Tempted to push the door open and maybe learn a little more about his daughter, he resisted.

He stopped in the act of opening his mouth to call Louise's name again. A sound. Sniffles.

His heart cracked, and he strode to the door on the left, putting his hand on the knob. Yeah, definitely sniffles. He forced himself to knock gently before pushing the door open.

His chest cramped and twisted at the sight of Louise on the bed, curled up in a ball, crying softly. He shouldn't be in her bedroom, and he knew it, but he couldn't stand the sight of her tears. Striding across the small room, he stopped at the side of the bed and said, "Louise?" gently, trying not to startle her.

Her head snapped up, her eyes wide and horrified. She rolled over, pulling the covers with her and covering her head. "Go away," came her muffled words.

What had happened? Last night, he'd been so close to kissing her. She'd even said out loud that she wanted him to, but he'd held off, determined to take it slow, to court her the way she deserved. Now today, she didn't even want to see him?

Hoping he wasn't making the second biggest mistake of his life, he slid into the bed behind her, spooning her back and hips, curving his legs to fit hers, keeping the blanket between them. His chest was against her back, and her head fit against his neck under his chin. He wrapped his arm around her waist and pulled her closer, pushing his other arm under her pillow so her head rested on his bicep.

She started crying in earnest then. Great, big hulking sobs that shook her body, his body, and the bed they lay on.

"Frig. What have I done?" he said softly, not really asking her but more asking himself. If he'd known sitting with her in church would produce this reaction, he never would have done it. Never. He'd have stood in the back. Outside, even, if it would have kept her from facing this pain, whatever it was that was making her cry.

He held her while she cried. She didn't try to get away. Grateful for that, because he would have let her go, he continued to hold her until her sobs became sniffles then hiccups.

Conscious that he shouldn't be there, that her family could come home at any time and he'd have a lot of explaining to do to her brother about why he was in her bedroom, especially after their history together, but he couldn't bring himself to get up. Not until he knew what the problem was.

He wanted to brush the tears off her cheeks, but he knew he'd better stay as still as possible. All the trouble they'd had last time had started with the emotions of him leaving. Everything had spiraled out of control from there. He couldn't even put a foot on that path, because he had less control around Louise than anywhere else in his life.

"Tell me, please," he begged softly when her hiccups had gotten fewer and far between.

She shook her head.

"Is it me?"

She didn't move. He supposed that was a yes.

"Did I do something?"

The covers moved as her head shook.

He took a breath to ask another question, but she moved, just a little. "I'm sorry. I've known that you're leaving again, and everything from the last time hit me like it was happening again, and I know you didn't do anything to deserve it, but I couldn't stand to go through it again, although this didn't help, and now you know, and I'm really embarrassed, because Norwegians don't cry."

She said it all in one breath and finally stopped to drag in a lungful of air. "I'm being a baby, I know it. And you haven't done anything wrong, and I'm sorry."

"Go with me," he said, still begging.

Her whole body stiffened. "What about Tella? We should just leave our home?"

Disbelief and fear laced her voice, but he wanted her with him more than he wanted anything else in the world. He couldn't let go now that the words were out of his mouth. "Yes. Both of you. Come with me."

"I can't live with you."

"No, of course not." He shoved his nerves down. "If there's not another condo available in my building, we'll rent something side by side. There are some great private schools. We'll send Tella somewhere with a great reputation. I owe you money, lots of it, anyway."

Her body relaxed a little. She was quiet for a long time. "What if I go and you decide you don't want to do 'us' anymore?" she asked.

It hurt, but it was a fair question. "I can get something set up with a lawyer to make sure you have your own money. Because of Tella, I owe you. You don't have to get a job. Even if you stay here, you don't have to work. You don't have to struggle."

"I never wanted you to feel like you have to take care of us."

"I want to take care of you."

"Can I think about it?" she finally asked.

His hand lay on her stomach, the blanket between them. He wanted to move it so much, but he forced himself to lay still. "I'm sorry I made you cry."

"It wasn't you."

"It's from what I did nine years ago."

She didn't deny it. He wondered how often over the years she'd cried alone. The thought ripped at his heart and hurt his stomach.

He wanted her to marry him. He wanted to spend the rest of his life making it up to her. He wanted to take care of her and never make her cry again. But she wasn't ready to trust him with all that. Would she ever be ready?

"I can't stay here," he finally whispered.

"No," she agreed, but she didn't move.

He didn't either.

"I have to go." He meant leave. His plane left this evening, and he should be on his way to the airport, but he didn't want to leave Louise. "Training camp is busy. Coach made us keep our phones in the locker room last year. I might only be able to call you in the evening when I get back and the morning before I go. I know as soon as I get there I'll get sucked into the busyness and everything, but I'll call."

Taking a big, shaky breath, Louise rolled to her back, and he moved a little to give her room. Her face was red and blotchy, her eyes swollen, her cheeks wet.

His entire being ached with her, but there was a little part of him that whispered she must feel something for him, since he could make her hurt like that.

He moved until he had both hands holding her face. He lay half over her and tried not to notice how soft and good she felt beneath him but focused on her eyes. "Look at me."

Her eyes fluttered open.

"I will call you. I promise."

A struggle went on in her eyes. He could almost see her jutting her chin out. "I believe you," she whispered, and he knew it cost her. Her mind would want to protect her heart, keep it from being broken by an ignorant man again, but her heart wanted to trust again, and she allowed it to win the fight. He hadn't deserved her trust the first time; he definitely didn't deserve it again, even as her face was still ravaged from the crying she'd just done over him.

He hesitated before he lowered his head, kissing her wet cheek as tenderly as he could. He had to be careful. Kissing Louise had never been an activity that was easy to stop.

Once he kissed her cheek, he moved to her swollen eyes, trying to soothe her with his lips, not knowing any other way. He kissed one closed eye then the other. Soft kisses. Her other wet cheek. Wet from tears she'd cried because of him. He fluttered his way down her angled jaw, feeling the soft skin, knowing there was a strong woman with backbone and purpose under it. One who would support him despite the opposition of the whole town, if necessary. A woman strong enough to forgive his stupidity and give him another chance. If she weren't, he wouldn't be here on her bed now.

His lips were on her neck, tasting the smooth skin there, when she moved a little, and her hand came out, sliding along his cheek with a sandpaper sound, loud next to his ear. His chest spasmed, and he squeezed his eyes closed against the urgent need to kiss her. Not yet. Instead, he trailed his lips up her neck and jaw, grabbing her earlobe and giving a light tug before moving across her cheekbone.

Her breathing had shifted with his, both more shallow. Their hearts raced together.

His lips moved to the tip of her nose, resting softly on it. Their eyes met and held. The air around them seemed to shimmer. His hands tingled, and he pushed them into her hair.

Her head tilted just a little, and his lips hung suspended in the air before they landed, whisper soft, on hers. Their eyes held, although his lids lowered halfway of their own accord, and it felt like they were shooting heated darts.

Her eyes flared as well, and her hand pulled on the back of his neck, urging him closer. He might have been able to win the battle with himself, but he couldn't fight her, too.

With a groan that felt like it had been torn from his soul, he angled his head and obeyed her unspoken command to be closer, meshing

JESSIE GUSSMAN

his lips with hers and kissing her the way he wanted to. The way he'd
dreamed about. The way he remembered.

Only the memories were a dim imitation to having the real Louise
under him again, his lips on hers, his hands touching the actual woman,
warm and soft. Everything he'd remembered and so much more.

It took three seconds before the door bursting open and hitting
the wall registered. Palmer's angry shouting penetrated his haze-filled
mind.

His eyes met Louise's startled ones before he was grabbed by both
shoulders and yanked from her bed. He stumbled to a knee, reaching
to see her around the bodies of her brothers.

"Didn't you learn anything from the last time?" Palmer shouted,
his face red, his hands clenched.

Ty didn't bother to answer. The fact that he was in her room, kissing
her, was answer enough. Even if that were the first kiss in nine years,
it didn't matter. If her brothers hadn't shown up, he might not have
stopped.

Even now, his lips were still tingling, and all he wanted was to see
her, touch her, and make sure she was okay.

He leaned farther, his knee burning from his weight pushing it
down into the old hardwood floor, but he needed to see that Louise
was fine. Needed one last reassurance of looking into her eyes and making sure she didn't regret what they'd just done, before her brothers
dragged him away and kicked him out of their house.

But Sawyer moved his body, and he couldn't lean around. He tried
the other direction, but Sawyer grabbed his shirt with both hands. "I
think you've put her through enough."

Palmer grabbed his own handful of Ty's shirt and shoved, pushing
him out Louise's door. "More than enough," he growled.

"Wait," Louise cried, but Palmer slammed the door closed with the
hand that wasn't shoving Ty away, down the hall. He half-expected to
be thrown down the stairs, too, and that was fine. He wasn't going to

fight Louise's brothers, but he needed to see her. Just once. Just to make sure she didn't think he was taking advantage of her with that kiss that he hadn't planned on but had rocked everything in his world. Brought back all the memories of the best and worst night of his life.

"Louise," he yelled. He *needed* to make sure she was okay. He kept his eyes glued to her closed door as they shoved him down the hall.

"Shut up," one of the brothers said.

Her door started to open. His heart leaped as her golden head came into view.

Then Palmer grabbed him and jerked him around. "Watch where you're going. I don't want to have to deal with the heartbroken females in this house if you fall down the stairs and break your sorry neck."

Each brother had an arm and a handful of his shirt, and they shoved him until he was out of the house and into his car.

"You know I'm coming back," he finally said as he sat behind the wheel. Louise was nowhere in sight.

"Do what you have to, but you grew up here, and you've not been away so long that you've forgotten it doesn't work the same way here that it does in the city. Louise isn't one of your one-night stands or a hookup or whatever the frig you're calling it today." Palmer's face was still red, but his tone had modulated a decibel or two.

Sawyer spoke in a more level tone, seeming more in control, but he didn't fool Ty. If someone was going to deck him, it would have been the quiet brother. "She survived what you did to her the last time. And she'll survive this, too. But if you love her, you're not going to put her through that kind of pain again."

"I asked her to go with me." His voice was rough with frustration.

Palmer threw his arms in the air. "Oh, that's just great. What an honor." His voice lowered and became a growl. "You have a child together. She deserves a ring."

Ty closed his eyes. "I know."

"I think if you knew that, you wouldn't have been in her room, lying on top of her. Get out of here," Sawyer said, his eyes fierce and dark.

Ty looked toward the house, but her brothers blocked his view. He'd call Louise on the way to the airport. In the meantime, at least he could say goodbye to Tella.

Chapter 21

Louise watched him pull out from the downstairs window. She knew her brothers were frustrated because they hadn't "protected" her the last time, and they felt it was their job.

It might have been nice if they'd asked her what she wanted before they threw Ty out, but she had to admit a part of her felt justified at what had just happened.

Ty had escaped unscathed nine years ago. And, yeah, he'd endured a little teasing and a few insults from the town since they'd found out, but it was nothing like what she'd lived through. Not that she wanted him to suffer since she had suffered. Nothing like that.

But to allow her brothers the privilege of throwing him out. Maybe she felt like it was okay.

If Ty was serious about her, he'd call. If he wasn't, if she didn't hear from him, well, he'd better not come back into town thinking he was going to get a third chance with her.

She had to let him see his daughter. She had no choice about that.

But this was the test. He'd left before, promising to call and come back and see her, and it had been lies. He had the opportunity to prove himself now.

She hoped he did, because she was really afraid she'd fallen for him. Again.

Fallen for him to the point where she'd give up any hope of inheriting a billion dollars and leave the home and land that she loved to move herself and her daughter to the city just so she could be near him.

ALL THE OTHER PASSENGERS were on the airplane and they were closing the door when Ty rushed into the boarding area. It wasn't a huge airport, and thankfully he'd been able to skim through security.

Unfortunately, he realized as he settled in his seat that he'd been in such a rush, so consumed with Louise and the feelings kissing her and leaving her had generated, that he'd never gotten his phone back from Tella.

His head dropped back against the seat, and he cursed his stupidity. If he'd remembered five minutes earlier, he would have missed his plane looking through the airport shops to see if he could find one that sold phones.

He'd pick one up in Pittsburgh as soon as he landed. He spent the flight itchy that he hadn't been able to contact Louise and find out how she was doing. How she'd handled the scene with her brothers.

He couldn't believe that she'd changed her mind about him, but it did nag him a little that she hadn't come to his defense, although he knew what her brothers had done to him was long overdue. Still, why didn't she come out? Had she felt like he was taking advantage of her? Maybe she hadn't been as overwhelmed by his kiss as he'd been by hers.

He tried to remember. He was pretty sure she was enjoying it, but he'd been so crazed by her taste and touch and finally kissing the woman he loved, he really couldn't say for sure.

But one thing he could say for sure was he loved Louise. Nothing he'd ever felt for anyone else even compared. He needed to tell her. Even if she didn't love him back, he wanted her to know how he felt. He should have told her before he left, instead of kissing her. Man, he was a dimwit sometimes.

It was after midnight when his plane finally landed in Pittsburgh, and there were no shops open to get a phone.

Training camp started at nine. He probably wouldn't be able to get a phone before. But he could get one of the trainers to pick one up. He couldn't leave the training facility, but they could.

He walked into his condo which felt cold and unwelcoming and lonely. He made sure his equipment was in order, took a quick shower, and fell into bed, only to toss and turn, worrying about what Louise thought since he'd left and hadn't called. His only consolation was that Tella must know that he didn't have his phone since he'd given it to her. With that thought came another: Louise might actually have his phone, which was perfect. It somehow made him feel satisfied in his soul that she might be holding something of his right now. It made the silence and the distance between them a little easier to bear.

He walked into training camp the next morning, and his mind most definitely was not on hockey.

Duncan Ross was the first teammate he saw. "Hey, let me borrow your phone, man," he said.

Duncan's eyebrows shot up. "Yeah, missed you too. Had a great off-season. Looking forward to the new season, and yep, maybe we can spend some extra time practicing," he said sarcastically, but he fished in his pocket for his phone, turning it on and punching in his passcode before handing it over.

Ty took the phone but almost immediately knew it was useless. "Crap." He grabbed his head like it hurt and bent over. "Crap, crap, crap."

Duncan was joined by Bobby and Nicklas. "What is it, dude? You having a seizure or something?"

"No." He jerked the phone back at Duncan. "Frig it. I don't know her frigging number. Or my mom's or anyone's. I just have them pro-grammed."

"Her?" Bobby caught the word immediately.

Something close to panic swirled in Ty's chest. He answered ab-sently, "Yeah."

"You fell in love over the off-season?" They laughed. "We'll see if it lasts." Nicklas smacked his shoulder. "Women want the glory, but they don't want the sacrifice that goes with it."

"Shut up," Ty said. He knew what Nicklas was saying, but that wasn't Louise at all.

"Just warning you, man. Never seen you with one that stuck, anyway. This one probably won't be any different. Especially if you don't call her for a day or two." Bobby snickered like it was funny. "They see your picture, and they think you're cheating."

Or that he'd left her again.

He didn't know what to do. He'd been planning on buying a new phone, but that wouldn't solve his problem, either. He could have a hundred phones, but if he didn't know her number... He knew his old house number, but his mom had turned it off. He didn't know her cell number. Heck, he didn't even know his own cell number.

He was screwed.

What was he going to do?

He flipped Duncan's phone end over end in his hand. The diner. He could call Patty. He brought the search app up and looked up "Sweet Water diner." Towns in twenty different states came up. What was the exact name? He couldn't remember. The panic and desperation fighting like a tempest inside him made it impossible to think. There had to be a way.

More guys were coming in; it was almost nine, and leaving wasn't an option. They filed into the meeting room, greeting each other after spending the summer apart. Seeing new faces. Not seeing some of the old ones.

Usually he loved the first day of camp. He loved pushing himself. The challenge. For the last few years, he'd been considered a leader on the team, and that was even better. He loved being able to share his knowledge and experience with the other guys.

They were told to put their phones away, and he pried his fingers off Duncan's phone and handed it back.

The day was misery. He actually ended up being reprimanded by the coach because he hadn't been paying attention. So unprofessional.

He'd never understood how some guys could come and not treat this like a serious job, putting in their all. But today, he got it. Louise was more important than even his job.

He didn't have any way of telling her that.

After camp that evening, they had the opportunity to meet the fans who were watching, sign autographs, and answer questions. Usually Ty took his time, staying for hours as he chatted with little boys who had big dreams, just like he did once.

But his heart wasn't in it. He needed to go and get a phone, to figure something out.

"You gotta get a hold of yourself, man," Duncan said as Ty stood in the locker room, racking his brain, trying to come up with a way to get Louise's number. "You've never been this tight. Is she really worth it?"

As he stared unseeing into Duncan's green eyes, he had an idea. "Hey, look up the number for my agent on your phone."

Duncan pulled his lip back but got his phone out and, after making sure of the name, looked it up.

"Let me borrow your phone. I need to call him."

"Sure. Just don't take too long. I get my kid for a couple hours tonight, and the ex gets mad if I'm late."

"Sure." Ty registered his words but didn't pay too much attention. The panic that stayed banked all day bubbled like lava in his chest.

"Hello?" his agent, Dave Smith, answered.

"Dave. Ty Hanson."

"Where have you been? I've been trying to call you since yesterday afternoon. I have an offer I need you to look over..."

"I need you to call my mother. I left home without my phone, and I need her to send it to me. Tell her to overnight it."

"Uh, yeah. I think I have her number. I can do that."

"Actually, have her send it to you. Get it to me as soon as it comes. Wherever I am."

"But Coach doesn't allow phones during camp."

"This is an emergency."

"I'll do what I can." He cleared his throat. "About this offer. It's a pretty good one."

Ty listened while Dave rattled off the figures. Any other time, he might have been amazed at the amount of money people were willing to offer him to play the game he loved. Used to love. It came in a far second to Louise and Tella.

"Yeah. That's fine."

"Don't do anything stupid until I get the final details hammered out. I'll have something for you to sign by the end of the week." He made a funny sound. "I have to go. Got some kind of stomach bug..." He made another strangled sound. "It's awful."

"I need my phone. Don't forget."

"I won't. Gotta go." His last words came out strangled and stiff before the line cut off abruptly.

Chapter 22

Louise dragged herself into work on Monday afternoon. Ty hadn't called. He hadn't texted. This could be high school all over again.

After the way he'd left her house on Sunday, she'd been almost sure he'd call her on the way to the airport or at least when he landed. Wouldn't he know she'd worry that he'd made it safely?

She tried to imagine the scenarios that would keep him from calling. Maybe his phone had died. Maybe he'd been busy getting his stuff ready for the season. Maybe he'd dropped his phone or lost it.

But she couldn't help remembering doing this exact same thing nine years ago when he'd left. Making excuses for him. Thinking the best. Holding on, even when it was obvious that he wasn't ever going to call. Or come home to see her.

"So, I heard about the hockey hunk that had his arm around you in church yesterday." Rebel smirked when she walked in.

"Same guy that's been hanging around here for the last few weeks." Louise shrugged like it was no big deal.

"Sitting together in church, as close as you two were reportedly sitting, is a big deal, and you know it." Rebel wiggled his brows, and Jackson laughed.

"Spill. When's the wedding?"

Louise's chest hurt with each beat of her heart, but she ignored their busybody questions and focused on doing her jobs. Both of them.

Ty had asked her to go with him. She wished she had just said yes. Then she'd know what was going on. But she couldn't believe that he'd do the same thing to her that he'd done before, so she kept her head up, deflected everyone's questions, and tried to stifle her doubts.

Tella came into the diner after school, since Miss Donna had gone on another trip to a craft show. She ate and did homework while Louise handled the supper rush.

Even though they were busy, the time seemed to drag until it was finally time to go home. She kept checking her phone. No texts. No calls.

Tempted to give up, she refused. Ty was going to keep his word. He did care for her. He couldn't kiss her the way he had and then walk away from her. But he'd done it before, a little voice insisted.

She sat at the kitchen table that evening, playing a board game with Pap and Gram and Tella. Ames and Palmer had gone on a four-wheeler ride after Louise got home and hadn't returned, so Louise helped the new nurse get Gram and Pap ready for bed, and then she and Tella went upstairs.

"Did Daddy call us?" Tella's question as she stopped in to say good night cracked Louise's heart.

Her mouth was dry, and she couldn't swallow. When did Tella start calling him Daddy? "Not yet. I'm sure the first day is busy. He probably should have gone home before he did." Maybe she shouldn't make excuses. Maybe she should just admit that he'd done what he'd done before. But she couldn't do that. Couldn't make Ty look less in Tella's eyes.

"If he calls later, will you tell him I said I love him?" Tella asked. Eyes that looked so much like Ty's stared at Louise over the covers.

"I will."

"And I miss him."

"Yeah. I'll tell him. I miss him too."

And she did. She'd had to bus her own tables. He hadn't been there with his hot eyes following her every move. She missed talking to him and just his comforting presence. A call would help.

But he didn't call that night. Nor the next day. Nor that night.

The forecast was calling for a fall blizzard, which wasn't unheard of this time of year, but Louise couldn't dredge up any feeling about it one way or the other as the folks around her talked about what a hard winter it was going to be.

By Wednesday, Louise knew she needed to quit deluding herself and face the truth: he'd done it again.

WEDNESDAY NIGHT AFTER camp, Ty was almost beside himself. He'd tried looking up numbers on the internet with no luck. Sweet Water must be the most common name in the United States.

He'd gone to the store yesterday after camp, hoping to buy a new phone and get his contacts and everything switched over, but he hadn't been able to provide his old phone or number, and due to some kind of glitch in their computer system, they'd not been able to access his account. He'd had to leave the store, because he'd been about two seconds from strangling the poor salesman who hadn't done anything wrong. The guy had shrugged and said, "Maybe try again in a couple of days when they work this bug out of the system."

Ty had tried using Duncan's phone to call what he thought were the right numbers. He'd tried about fifty different combinations, getting the wrong number every time. He'd also harassed Dave, who was still really sick, but Dave claimed he couldn't get a hold of his mother. Ty remembered she had a trip planned for this week, but she should have her cell phone on her.

Ty toyed with the idea of going AWOL from camp and taking the first plane he could get to North Dakota. If he didn't have a phone by tomorrow, that's what he was going to do.

"Hey, Ty! Yo, man, wait!" Duncan hollered.

Ty turned to see him waving his phone and jogging down the hall toward him.

"It's your agent. Now, apparently, I'm your secretary. I want a raise."

"Gimme the phone." Ty reached for it, hoping he had news about his mother or his phone or something.

"I'm gonna start charging you for using my phone," Duncan complained but handed the phone over.

"Yeah?" Ty said into the mouthpiece.

"Ty. Your mother finally answered her phone. I guess she didn't recognize my number and thought I was a telemarketer. She doesn't have her voicemail set up." Dave's voice was still weak. He'd told Ty he'd spent the entire week in bed and hadn't been able to keep anything but clear liquids down.

Ty knew his mother wasn't very tech savvy, so it didn't surprise him that she didn't have voicemail. "Okay?" Just tell him about his phone already.

"She said she mailed it, like priority mail or something, on Tuesday. She gave me the numbers, and it's supposed to come tomorrow. I know you're real concerned about it. I can go to your apartment and hang out there until it comes if you want me to."

"Yeah. I want it as soon as it comes. Wherever I am. I don't care about the box or the packaging or anything. Just get me the phone."

"Okay. I'll have that contract for you to look over, then, too."

"Fine," he clipped out. He really didn't care about the contract.

Dave groaned a little, and Ty felt bad for him for being sick all week. Not bad enough to tell him not to worry about the phone.

Friday after camp, Dave sat on a chair in the hall outside of the locker room. Ty saw him immediately when he walked out and rushed over. Guilt slapped at his insides because Dave really did look like the walking dead. Pasty white face, sunken cheeks, and big black circles under his eyes. He was dressed in beige slacks and a polo shirt, and they both looked like they were a size too big.

He held his head in his hands, and his whole posture screamed defeat. Ty assumed the folder sitting on his legs was his contract, but he didn't see his phone anywhere.

"Dave." Ty stopped in front of him.

Dave slowly raised his head. His eyes were wary, and Ty didn't need a crystal ball to see that it wasn't just his sickness. Dave had bad news.

"What?" Ty snapped out.

"I was sick on the way in."

"Sorry to hear that." Ty tried to inject compassion into his voice, but he was afraid he failed miserably.

"I puked in the men's room toilet." Dave nodded at the restrooms to their left.

Ty almost said he really didn't want the details of his sickness, just hand the phone over, but he forced himself to cling to a thread of decency and manners. Louise would want him to act like a civil human being. "I'm sorry to hear that."

"I had your phone in my hand."

The past tense of that sentence concerned him. His stomach began to undulate.

"It fell in the toilet."

Ty swore. Then he glanced around. His eyes were probably wild, but he didn't even care. "Where is it now?"

"Still there." Dave put a hand over his stomach. "I just couldn't..."

Well, Ty could. Maybe the thing was waterproof. He'd paid enough for it; it should survive a shark attack.

"Which stall?" he asked as he walked away.

If Dave answered, Ty didn't hear. He yanked the bathroom door open and walked in. He'd never been in that bathroom—the locker rooms were right beside it—but it was typical. A few urinals and two stalls. The first toilet had puke in it. Other things floated in it as well, but Ty didn't even hesitate. He couldn't see his phone, but he stuck his hand in anyway, swirling it around until he felt the hard plastic.

Grabbing it, he yanked it out, rinsed it off in the sink, soaping it up along with his hands, and carefully dried it off.

He remembered hearing they shouldn't be turned on when wet and sticking it in rice was supposed to draw moisture out. He could wait two more hours, he figured as he rushed out of the bathroom.

"Here," Dave called, waving the folder.

"Thanks," Ty ground out as he grabbed the folder. Manners, and the thought of what Louise would think, made him ask if he needed help up.

Dave stood on wobbly legs.

Concern for the man that had become a friend hit him as Dave swayed on his feet. "I think you ought to go to the hospital. You're probably dehydrated."

"Yeah. My wife wanted me to go this morning, but I told her I needed to get your phone first."

Ty cursed to himself. How could he walk away after the man had delayed the treatment he needed just to get him his phone? Although, in hindsight, it would have been better if the phone were sitting in a box beside his condo door.

Five hours later, Dave was admitted to the hospital, his wife was with him, and Ty walked into his condo, holding a bag of rice he'd picked up at the grocery store because he didn't have any in his condo. His phone was already buried in it.

He paced. How long did the phone need to stay in the rice? It had already been in about thirty minutes. More?

He gave it another five before digging it out and holding his breath while he held the button on the side.

Nothing.

Maybe it was dead. He brought his charger out from his bedroom, plugging it into his phone then sticking it in the wall socket. Electricity arced, stinging his fingers and arm before the lights in his apartment flickered and went out.

Right.

If his phone wasn't already dead from being dropped in the toilet, he'd just killed it.

That settled it for him. He grabbed his wallet and keys and, on a whim, the folder with the new contract and walked out, locking the door behind him.

Chapter 23

Louise glanced out one of the windows as the early October blizzard put the snow down. Ames and Palmer were out taking care of the stock. They didn't quite have everything ready for winter, and they were working to make sure they didn't lose anything in the freak storm.

Twenty-two inches. They hadn't gotten that much snow in October since 1972. At least Friday was her day off, and she wasn't driving in it. Although she kind of wished she were working. It would keep her mind busy. As it was, she had finished up all her editing projects and played two hours' worth of games with Tella and Gram and Pap.

Now the three of them were watching a movie on her laptop while vegetable soup simmered on the stove, bread rose on the counter, and Louise tore down the pantry, emptying it out, wiping the shelves, and organizing everything in alphabetical order. It wasn't helping get her mind off the thing she was trying not to think about. Her silent phone.

She almost dropped a ten-pound bag of flour when it buzzed. Throwing the flour on the shelf with the "D" items, she grabbed her phone from her pocket with trembling hands.

Hope withered in her chest when Paul's number came up. She almost didn't answer. But she swiped on and said, "Hello?"

"Louise. Hey. How have you been?"

"Just fine, Paul. Thanks."

"I heard about you and that hockey player in church last Sunday."

From the way he talked, he wasn't there, which she'd never even noticed. "That's nice."

"You two getting married soon?"

"No. We're not getting married." Louise said it firmly and clearly. She was tired of answering questions. Although the hardest questions to face were Tella's. She hadn't asked today yet if "Daddy" had called. Yesterday when she asked, she'd called him "Ty," and Louise hadn't been able to correct her.

"I was thinking about you, and I know he left without a word the last time. If you're interested in renegotiating our agreement, just let me know."

She wanted to snap Paul's head off, but how could she get angry when he was just stating the facts? That's what Ty did last time.

Controlling her voice, she said very clearly, "Thanks, but while Ty and I do not have marriage plans, we are still together."

"Oh." His voice dropped. "I just heard on the news that he had disappeared, and I thought you two had broken up."

"He disappeared?" Louise repeated before realizing that if she and Ty were "together" like she'd indicated, she'd know about that.

"It's what the news said." There was a deliberate pause. "You don't know anything about it?"

"I have to go. Sorry, Paul." She hung up and pulled up the search engine on her phone, intending to search for hockey news, but the internet was down. Not uncommon in a storm like this.

Frustrated and more than a little worried, she dialed Donna's number.

"Hello?"

"Miss Donna. It's Louise."

"Yes, I have your name programmed in."

"Have you heard from Ty?"

"Today?"

"Yes." Louise bit her tongue, because the way Miss Donna said "today" sounded like Ty had been in touch with his mother at some point.

"No. Why?"

"I just wondered." She didn't want to worry Donna about Ty disappearing, especially if Paul were making it up. Surely if Ty had gone missing, his mother would know.

Miss Donna continued, "I know his agent was sick and Ty was at the hospital with him last night. Apparently, it was a nasty stomach bug."

"Oh. I hope Ty doesn't get it," Louise said, knowing her voice wasn't as strong and confident as she wanted it to be, but she couldn't help it. Obviously, Ty was just fine and talking to his mother. But he hadn't taken the time to call her. Her stomach felt like a ball of wire had landed in it. "I'm sorry, Donna. I need to go. Thanks." She hung up before Donna could say anything else.

Although her heart felt like it was on fire, and her stomach felt scratched and sore, her eyes were dry, thankfully. No more tears.

Still, part of her refused to believe that Ty had not been sincere when he'd lain on her bed and spoken all the sweet words to her. He wouldn't abandon his daughter, either. Suddenly she wished she'd spent more time on the phone with Miss Donna and questioned her more thoroughly, no matter that she was embarrassed Miss Donna might find out Ty hadn't called or texted her since he left.

Louise put the pantry back together but couldn't calm her restless spirit, so she tackled the back porch, scrubbing and cleaning until it sparkled.

Saturday, there was still no word. The snow had stopped, and Louise made it into the diner where work was slower than usual. She didn't sleep very well that night and was almost late for church. It was hard to get the gumption to play, but she did her best because it was her job, anticipating the moment when she could step off the platform and sink down into her pew. Alone. So different than last week.

There seemed to be more talking than usual during the offertory, but Louise didn't try to look around. She always lost her place in the music when she took her eyes off it, and she couldn't see much from the corner where the piano was anyway. Plus, she just couldn't find it in herself to care.

Finally, she stepped off the platform as Pastor gave the references and people's Bibles started crinkling as they found their places.

Louise kept her head down and was almost beside her row before she saw him. Sitting in her seat. Same position as last week. His arm over the back rest, her purse and Bible beside him. His eyes tracking her every movement.

She couldn't help it. She stopped dead in the aisle. He wasn't smiling. But maybe his eyes were pleading with her to have patience or maybe to believe in him. Whatever it was, she couldn't deny him. Did that make her weak? Maybe.

Whatever.

She slid into her seat, stopping where she had the last time. This time, he didn't say anything but moved her purse and Bible and slid over, putting his arm on her shoulder and tucking her against him.

Maybe it was Palmer growling low and deep behind them or maybe someone's stomach was rumbling.

Louise didn't care. She wasn't sure what had kept Ty away, but until she could grill him, she was just going to be glad to be beside him again.

The church service dragged on and on. Usually Louise loved to listen to Pastor explain God's Word and exhort believers to love and good works, but today she just wanted him to finish.

There was no dinner on the grounds, and by the time she was done playing the postlude, Ty stood by the platform stairs waiting for her.

"Ride with me, please. I need to talk to you."

"Tella..."

"Is going to spend the afternoon with her grandmother and the evening with me, if that's okay with you."

He took her hand, his feeling big and strong next to her slender fingers, but as he turned around, Palmer and Sawyer blocked their path, standing shoulder to shoulder.

"You haven't called her since you left." Palmer stated it flatly. It wasn't a question. Louise wasn't sure how he knew, unless Tella had been talking to him.

The people milling around in the church building quieted. No one pretended to not be staring at the Old Testament-type confrontation at the altar.

"No." Ty pulled his hand from hers and pushed his shoulder in front of her as though she needed protection from her own brothers. Which was ridiculous.

Chapter 24

Ty faced Louise's brothers. At the front of the church of all places. He didn't want to fight them and didn't plan to. If they felt it was necessary to deck him, then he supposed he deserved it, if for nothing else than being dumb as dirt. But he didn't want Louise to get hurt, so he put her behind him.

"And you don't have anything more to say about that?" Sawyer asked menacingly.

"Quit it, you two."

Ty almost fell over at Louise's voice behind him.

She stepped around him. "Let him alone."

"We're not letting him get away with this again." Palmer didn't move and barely looked at his sister. "Tella said he didn't call all week. I know the guy can use a phone. Apparently, he's the type that's out of sight, out of mind."

Ty clenched his jaw. That's not the way it was, but he couldn't expect anyone here, least of all Louise, to believe him.

Silence descended.

Then Louise spoke, her voice quiet but strong. "You're wrong. He's not like that. There's an explanation. You just need to give him a chance."

Ty quit facing her brothers. His shoulders relaxed. Louise was defending him? After everything he'd done, and how he'd not managed to contact her all week, she was still defending him? He looked at her in wonder.

"Really? You believe that?" he asked.

She turned to him. "Am I wrong?"

He shook his head slowly. "I left my phone here, with Tella. She was looking at the pictures. My mom took it, and Tella didn't realize that I never got it."

"You didn't have your phone all week?" Louise asked softly.

He shook his head. "It gets worse. I couldn't remember anyone's number, even my own. I couldn't get a phone from the store, my agent's been sick, and when my mom finally sent the phone, when my agent got it, he dropped it in the toilet as he was throwing up."

Louise's face scrunched up.

"That was the last straw, but I had to take him to the hospital because he was dehydrated from being so sick. I didn't even tell the coach I was skipping practice Friday, I just left and caught the first plane out of Pittsburgh, which didn't come directly to North Dakota but had a layover in Chicago. Then I had a two-day delay because of the storm. I just got in and drove straight from the airport to here."

Her mouth hung open, but she wasn't smiling.

He flexed his hands. "I'm sorry." The knot in his throat made his words rough. "I was going crazy all week not being able to talk to you." He searched her eyes. "I can't do it again. If you won't come to Pittsburgh with me, I'm retiring today. I've already made a deal with Mom to buy the ranch." If only she would say something, but her expression hadn't changed. "Will you take me if I'm a rancher, Louise?"

Her eyes widened.

Yeah. He might as well jump in with both feet. He took her hand. "I don't have a ring. I don't even have a phone right now. But marry me, Louise. Please?"

A sigh echoed through the church. Ty blinked and looked around. The entire congregation, including Pastor Houpe, stared at them. Sawyer's face still looked serious, but Palmer had a twinkle in his eye.

"Say something, Louise."

"Yes." It was soft and low, but it was the right word.

His lips curved up as a cheer erupted from the watching congregation.

"Yes," she said, louder and more clearly.

He put his arms around her, lifting and turning in a circle. Nothing that entire week had gone as he'd planned. But somehow, Louise was in his arms, and she'd just agreed to marry him. It made everything worthwhile.

He felt a light touch on his arm. Looking down, he saw Tella. She gave him a tentative smile. Keeping one arm around Louise, he put the other around his daughter. It wouldn't be long before they would all be a real family.

Later that afternoon, after he'd gotten a shower and played a few games at the table with Tella and his mother and Louise, his mother took Tella into the kitchen to help make supper since Georgia and Ford were coming. Ty sat on the couch with Louise pressed close to his side.

"I was serious about quitting hockey."

"I don't want you to give up something like that for me. You love it."

He dipped his head down so that their eyes met. "I love you more."

Her eyes widened. He grinned because she hadn't been expecting that.

"I love you, too," she whispered.

"I know." He knew he sounded cocky.

Sure enough, her eyes narrowed.

"I'm serious. As soon as you saw me sitting in your pew, and you hesitated, then you came and sat down beside me...I knew then that you loved me."

She gave a short laugh.

"It's true. When you hesitated, I knew you were angry. And rightly so, but I gave you the chance to humiliate me in front of the whole church." He paused and said softer, "Like I humiliated you." He pulled a breath in through his nose. "Yet you didn't. And if I wasn't sure then,

I was completely sure when you defended me to your brother without even knowing what had happened this week and why I didn't call."

"I can't say I never doubted," she said honestly, and he loved her for that. "But every time I doubted, I just couldn't give up all hope."

He kissed her forehead, and she turned her face up. He half-laughed, half-groaned. "Kissing you is hazardous to my sanity."

"Mine too." Her smile matched his.

He touched his lips gently to hers, pulling back almost immediately as sparks shot through him at the simple touch. "You said you'd marry me." He looked in her eyes. "How soon?"

"As soon as you want to."

"Tomorrow?"

He didn't expect her whispered, "Okay."

"No, it takes a good nine or twelve months to plan a nice wedding. We can have something grand with all the bells and whistles."

"I'm not a bells and whistles kind of girl."

He pressed his lips together, nodding. She wasn't. Not for herself, anyway.

Pressure pushed in. Pressure because he was supposed to be at training camp early tomorrow morning, and he'd already missed Friday without even telling Coach he wouldn't be there. If he were going to play, if he were going to get the contract, he needed to get back. But he didn't want to leave Louise.

"I can retire from hockey. If you don't want to be in Pittsburgh, we'll get married and take over the ranch. Mom hasn't offered a contract renewal to the guys who are renting our land. We can start in the spring."

"What do you want?"

"I have a season left on my contract, and I actually have my new contract lying around here somewhere."

"So, you want to keep doing hockey?" she asked with a lift of her brow.

He pulled her a little closer, knowing that she was way more than hockey to him, and if he had to choose, he'd choose her. But in his heart, he loved the game and knew it was a rare privilege to be where he was.

"Yeah."

Her head moved up and down firmly.

A car pulled in.

"That must be Georgia and Ford." He pursed his lips. "Can we look at my contract after dinner?"

"Of course."

Georgia showed up alone. Ty supposed he should have figured, since Ford rarely, if ever, left his ranch, although their mother insisted he'd been to her house to eat a few times.

He supposed it didn't matter, but he was on the top of the world and wanted to share his news with everyone.

They started out talking about Georgia's month-long trip to Europe. "How soon do you leave?" Ty asked.

"In two weeks." Georgia's face was shining. "I've always wanted to see the castles and old buildings and visit Norway. I've been told all my life I'm such a Norwegian, but I've never even been to Norway. I want to see the land of my ancestors."

As tiny and dark as she was, she was definitely a throwback, but he didn't rub it in. "You should have told me. I could have helped you out with a trip like that."

"It's better that I've saved the money myself." Georgia grinned. "Plus, it's not easy dealing with Ford every day. Maybe the desire to go to Europe has gotten stronger, the more time I've spent with him."

Ty laughed a little. His eyes were on Tella. "I was just curious when you were going to be gone because Louise and I are going to get married."

Tella's head jerked up from her plate of fried potatoes and hamburger. Her eyes, the same eyes that stared back at him in the bathroom mirror every morning, were bright. She looked first to Louise, who sat beside him at the table. He had his arm around her and ate with one hand, like he just couldn't bear to stop touching her. After the week he'd had, it was the honest truth.

Then Tella looked at him. "You did it."

"Told you I was going to."

"What's that about?" Louise asked.

"He told me he wanted to marry you, but he needed some time to talk you into it."

"You two were conspiring against me?"

"Nope," Ty said. "It was for you, since I'm such a catch."

His sister snorted, and Louise rolled her eyes. After what he'd put her through, it was a wonder she didn't dump her plate on his head for that smart comment, but she didn't.

His mother beamed.

Georgia's mouth hung open. "You're giving up hockey?"

"I can be married and still play hockey. I've got a contract around here somewhere for another six years." He looked around, wondering where he'd set it. "Not to brag, sis, but it's one of the biggest contracts ever offered in the history of hockey."

"A billion dollars?" Georgia asked skeptically.

Under his hand, Louise stiffened. His head jerked around to her, but she was staring at her plate, pushing the food around with her fork.

"No. Of course not." His answer was for Georgia, but he was staring at Louise. Why had Georgia's question caused her distress?

"What's up with the billion dollars?" His eyes lasered in on his sister.

She lifted a shoulder. "Louise doesn't get it if you don't live here in North Dakota." She stated it matter-of-factly, like it was something he should know.

Louise's head was still down, but his mom looked as confused as he felt.

Georgia paused with a spoonful of potatoes halfway to her mouth. Her gaze took in Louise then him. His puzzled look. "Oh," she said. "I'm sorry, Louise. I assumed you'd told him."

"No."

"It's kind of a big deal," Georgia said. "I never thought you wouldn't tell him."

"Tell me what?" Ty asked, starting to get frustrated.

Louise looked up but still didn't meet his gaze. "I got a letter a few months ago. Palmer got the same thing, and it's legit."

"And?" he prompted, feeling the back of his neck tighten. He hated it when it did that. It always meant bad news.

"And it said that I was to inherit a billion dollars."

Ty sat stunned. "I had no idea. That's fantastic." But she wasn't smiling.

"There were a few stipulations."

"Like?"

"Like I had to get married."

He got it immediately. "That's why you were with Paul."

She nodded. "A little."

"But you'll still get it if we get married?"

"It doesn't matter who I marry, but I have to be married by Christmas, and we have to settle in North Dakota in order for me to inherit the money. If we ever move out of the state, barring a doctor's order, we forfeit the money and have to pay it back." Louise finally met his gaze.

Ty's lungs pushed out all the air that was in them. "You didn't think to mention this to me?" he asked slowly.

"I did. But I didn't want you to have to choose between hockey and me getting money."

"You were going to give up a billion dollars so I could keep playing hockey?"

"You're good at what you do, and you love it."

He couldn't quite comprehend the magnitude of what Louise had been willing to do.

She tilted her head. "There's a contract lying around here." She smiled a little at using his words. "It's one of the biggest in hockey history. And it's yours. You earned it, and I don't want to take that away."

"But you could have a billion dollars."

"It'd be about half that once they took the taxes out."

He rolled his eyes. "Five hundred million is nothing to sneeze at."

Uncertainty crept into her eyes. "I'd rather be with you."

He couldn't doubt it. Not with the fact staring him right in the face that she'd been willing to give up a fortune for him. Literally.

It was then that he knew what he had to do.

Chapter 25

"You realized we've never actually been out on a date?" Ty asked his new wife.

The wedding ceremony had gone beautifully. Both of Louise's brothers had stood up with them along with Georgia and Tella. Ford hadn't come. They were going to visit him Monday when they went back to Sweet Water and picked up Tella from his mother's place in town and headed out on their honeymoon.

They were going to see the Grand Canyon and figured they wanted Tella with them.

They were spending the next three nights on Ty's new ranch, his old home. It's where Louise wanted to stay.

"Does that make us less married?" Louise asked with a little smile from the passenger side of his truck he'd bought in the last week.

"No." Their clasped hands sat on the console between them. As far as he knew, the wedding ceremony was going strong back in Sweet Water. They'd stayed an hour. Which was an hour longer than either of them wanted to. He was sure about this because after the wedding Louise had whispered that she was ready to go. His heart hadn't stopped its frantic pumping since her breath had tickled his ear.

"But just mark down that I owe you. I can't believe I'm married to a woman who has never been on a date."

"Maybe that's because the man I wanted to date was busy elsewhere." She grinned at him as she said it, and he knew she wasn't holding that against him, but it still sent pangs of guilt up his arm.

He'd announced his retirement from hockey this past week. It hadn't been as hard as he'd thought it might be. He would always love the game. But it wasn't even a choice that he'd agonized about. Louise was more important. The first week of training camp, when he couldn't talk to her, had shown him that. And she'd given up so much for him, had been willing to give up so much more. A billion dollars. She'd rather have him than a billion dollars. Hockey was easy to give up when he considered what Louise was willing to do. Had done. Maybe they'd have some boys who would play.

That thought made his chest squeeze and he looked at Louise as the truck pulled to a stop in front of their new home. The papers for the house weren't signed, but they were scheduled to go to the lawyer's in two weeks and take care of it.

"What?" she asked.

"I want a boy," he said.

Her eyes widened and her cheeks got a little red, but she didn't drop her eyes. "Four boys."

He blinked. "Think I'm gonna need to add on to the house."

"And four girls."

"Never mind, we'll just live in the barn."

She laughed. If she were nervous about tonight, it didn't show. He had the feeling she wasn't nervous, she was eager.

He, on the other hand, was extremely nervous. He hadn't had a butterfly revolt of this magnitude in his stomach since his first professional hockey game. And even then it wasn't this bad.

"Why am I so nervous?" he asked, glancing at Louise, before opening his door and walking around. His hand shook as he pulled the latch on her side and opened her door.

"You don't need to be nervous. We can lock my brothers out tonight." She took his hand and he helped her down.

The air had a definite chill, so they hurried into the house.

In the past week, they'd redone his parents' bedroom. They'd also gotten Tella's room ready for her.

He thought his dad would be mostly happy about how things had turned out. He'd gotten his degree, which had been so important to his father. And his dad would have approved of Louise. More than approved. He would have loved Tella, too.

Louise hadn't bothered with the whole big, white dress. She'd worn a pretty blue one that was fitted around the waist and had a skirt that flirted with her legs with every step she took.

He hung his coat up and helped Louise take hers off. His trembling hands would barely allow him to hand it up. It didn't help that she stood right beside him and waited.

"Hungry?" he asked. She hadn't eaten much at the reception.

She shook her head.

He allowed his hands to slide around her waist. "I've wanted to hold you since I saw you walking down the aisle."

Her hands slid up his chest and out his shoulders. He hadn't bothered with a suit or tie. He only wore a button up and her hand trailed heat right through it.

"You definitely have broader shoulders than you did in high school." She leaned forward and placed her lips on his shoulder through the material of his shirt. "I like them." Her voice was soft and breathy.

"Come here." He pulled her closer. She lay her head on his chest and they swayed slowly together, like they were dancing, but there was no music.

"I'm sorry we missed so much." He could have spent the last nine years with her.

"Let's don't look back."

Her curves fit perfectly against his body. He couldn't help running his hands up and down her back, feeling the flare of her hips, the dip of her waist.

"I think that's a good idea." He ran his fingers up her slender neck. "Am I allowed to take this down." He touched her hair.

Her fingers left his shoulders. He slid his hands down and held her waist to him while she pulled out whatever was holding it up and shook it out. It tumbled around her shoulders and down her back, releasing the scent of flowers and vanilla.

He buried his nose and a hand in it. "Pretty," he murmured. "Soft, too."

Her hands slid around his waist. He closed his eyes.

They'd been slowly moving, just a little more than swaying, really, and he hadn't been paying attention. So when his leg bumped the couch, he wasn't expecting it and lost his balance. He managed to twist and they landed together, him on his back, her lying on top of him.

"I didn't plan that, but I like it." Her hair spilled down around them and her body felt perfect resting on his.

Their legs were tangled in her swishy skirt, and she put her hand on his chest, resting her chin on top of it.

"I like it too," she said softly.

"Eight kids?" he said, going back to their earlier conversation. "Maybe we should have talked about this. Do you have any other surprises for me?"

"I don't. But I think I saw Pastor putting your name down for every festival the town has once he learned your were retiring from hockey." She stretched up and kissed the cleft in his chin.

"As long as he put yours with it, I'm okay with that."

"I gave Patty my two week notice on Monday." She wiggled up, and he groaned softly. She kissed his neck.

Her lips were soft and warm and better than anything. He had trouble remembering they were in the middle of a conversation. "That's good, because I have big plans for you."

"Big plans?" she asked before her teeth nipped his ear. Her hands threaded though his short hair.

"I have a lot of kissing to do," he murmured, the fire that was always there between them had flamed to life.

"Mmm." She trailed her lips across his cheek. "Sounds important. Maybe we'd better get started."

Her lips touched his and all the sensations he remembered from before came roaring back. Only this time he didn't have to worry about stopping. He could kiss her all night if he wanted.

She lifted her head enough for him to suck in a breath. "I love you," he panted.

"I love you too," she replied. He knew it was true.

Epilogue

Ford kept the sitting room dark and his over-sized hoodie pulled up and over his head as Georgia led Ty and his new wife in. He hated people seeing his face. The eyepatch was enough to put most folks off. But the puckered and ugly scars where half of a handsome face used to be downright scared folks. Especially children. And ladies with queasy stomachs. Louise was a hardy North Dakota girl, but that didn't mean she wouldn't be put off by his ugliness.

Ford hadn't gone to the wedding. So Ty had brought his new wife here to meet him.

Like he even needed to. They might only live forty-five minutes away, but Ford wasn't planning on dropping in for coffee. Or Christmas. Or anything in between.

Maybe once upon a time, he enjoyed visits and company, games and friends, but with half his face and most of his leg missing, he was the freak at any party.

Keeping the lights dim helped a little. The hoodie gave him protection as well.

Georgia walked confidently in. She knew him, and her eyes went immediately to the corner where he always stood. The deepest shadows in the room.

His little brother walked in next, his arm around a pretty blond who would have to be Louise, of course. A bit of jealousy, mean and snickering, crawled up his throat. He swallowed to shove it back down. He'd be happy for his brother. Even if there was no chance in the world that, even with all his millions, he'd ever have a beautiful wife by his side.

Ty held their daughter's hand on his other side. A cute little girl.

COWBOYS DON'T HAVE A SECRET BABY

Ford was an uncle. That had been a shock he was still getting used to.

"Ford, they can't see you when you stand back in the corner like that." Exasperation laced Georgia's voice. He'd hired her to help him with his home and business. She did a great job. But she didn't put up with his crap. Not even a little.

Georgia might be small, but she was a powerhouse. She'd make him move forward. Better to do it on his own.

Too bad she was leaving next week. At least she'd hired his replacement. The cow-eyed daughter of Mr. and Mrs. Nelson. She was younger than him, and he'd specifically asked Georgia for an old woman or a man, but he'd known Mr. and Mrs. Nelson growing up and kind of remembered their daughter, Morgan, from a few basketball games when their schools had played together.

Morgan had been ugly as a mud fence and blind as a bat with glasses at least an inch thick perched on her stub of a nose. She'd been fat, too. Her hair so light blond as to be almost white and so thin one could see her scalp under it. She also had some kind of skin condition that gave her red welts all over her face. Like him, her looks had made her memorable. Not in a good way. She wasn't the right age—he'd wanted an older woman—but she'd do.

He shoved his cowboy hat down and took one step to the edge of the shadow.

"This is my wife and daughter, Ford." Ty's voice jerked his thoughts back to the present. That was the trouble with being alone so much. One had a tendency to forget the social niceties like paying attention to people when they were standing in front of one.

"Quit scowling," Ty said. "You're not going to intimidate them."

Louise held her hand out. "We've met, but it's good to see you again."

Ford smirked and reached out to shake her hand. He'd lost his pinky and ring fingers on his right hand, and people's faces when he shook with them were comical to watch.

He could laugh. After all, God was laughing at him. He still had the third finger on his left hand, like he'd ever find a woman who wanted to put a ring there.

But Louise wasn't like every other person. She peered into the gloom to try to meet his eye while her hand took his in a firm grip. Not the pansy grip most people used when they saw he was physically disabled. Like he even wanted that label. He never used it. He knew what it was like to be whole and handsome, and he hadn't accepted that it wasn't him anymore.

"Ty loves you, and he talks a lot about you."

Ford snorted. They'd barely even talked since their dad died. No, since his accident. They had a lot of good memories up to that point. Okay, they talked every week, but he didn't tell anyone about the bitterness in his heart.

Ford didn't miss the way Ty pulled his new wife closer, tucking her next to him like he couldn't stand for there to be any air between them. It didn't surprise him, though. If Ty loved the woman so much that he'd retire from hockey, and at the beginning of the season, giving up the biggest contract ever offered to a player in the history of the sport, to become a rancher, because that must be what his wife wanted? Yeah. His brother was in love.

Good luck with that. In Ford's experience, girls were fickle and catty. Shauna had broken up with him while he was still in the hospital recovering from the farm accident. He was missing a leg, half his face, and a couple of fingers, and she took his confidence with her as she walked out of the hospital room after letting him know she wasn't doing the nursemaid thing for the rest of her life. Like he had a catheter bag she'd have to empty or something.

Georgia invited everyone to sit down, but Ty declined, to Ford's relief.

"We're heading out on our honeymoon."

"You're taking her on your honeymoon?" Ford probably shouldn't have asked, but the question slipped out as he looked aghast at Tella.

Ty tugged her closer, and she put her arms around his waist while his hand landed in the center of her back, hugging her against him. "I've missed a lot of time with her, and I want to try to make it up. She'll love seeing the Grand Canyon, anyway."

Ford shrugged. Whatever.

"Then we're coming back and living on the ranch. Just because we bought it doesn't mean you can't come back and visit as much as you want," Ty said.

Not that Ford would want to. There were too many good memories of being with his dad there. Plus that one really bad memory that he'd wished every day since he could change. Go back and make one different decision, and he'd still be handsome and whole. Impossible, of course.

He could admit to himself, though, that he probably wouldn't be a millionaire if he'd not been in the accident.

But no amount of money could give him back his limbs. At this point, he could afford plastic surgery on his face, but he didn't want to go under the knife again. There was no guarantee he'd look better anyway, and he'd never look the way he pictured himself in his mind.

"Yeah, I'll have to do that," he said, since Ty seemed to be waiting on an answer. He had no intention of visiting, but he didn't want to upset everyone by being so blunt.

See? He could be kind.

"Well, we're headed out. We'll stop in on our way home." Ty moved forward and grabbed Ford in a hug. Ty might be more muscular now, but Ford was taller. That's all he had going for him, since he couldn't compete in the looks department.

But his brother's hug felt strong and good, reminding him of his father. "I wish you the very best," Ford said and meant it with everything in his heart.

Thanks so much for reading! To join Jessie's newsletter to receive updates on her writing, news about Jessie and information on upcoming releases, click HERE[1].

To read Ford's story, the next book in the Sweet Water Ranch Billionaire Cowboy series, click HERE[2].

Keep reading for a sneak peek of the first chapter in Ford's story.

CHAPTER 1

"I can't wear this," Morgan Nelson said with one arm crossed over her chest where the see-through material left nothing, truly nothing, to the imagination.

People shouted and swore, their voices echoing in the large room broken only by portable racks of clothes and a few flimsy partitions. Tangy sweat, bold perfume, and that familiar scent of nervousness combined together in a familiar, though unloved, scent mixture.

"We're in the middle of a show. We don't have time for drama queens." Henrique Ove barely looked up from where he was placing duct tape in strategic locations on another model's outfit to keep it in place.

"I'm not being a drama queen." Please. Morgan did everything she was asked to do, and more, with not a word of complaint. Not about the long hours. Not about the near-starvation diet. Not about the hideous outfits that no normal person would wear. As long as they paid her, she'd wear whatever they set out.

But she didn't sign up to do a nude.

---

1.   https://dl.bookfunnel.com/qx71qtunbm

2.   https://www.amazon.com/gp/product/B07QKW4XCQ/ref=series_dp_rw_ca_3

"This was not in my preshow outfits. I did not have this in practice yesterday." She'd tried every one on, and multiple assistants had made sure that everything fit and was shown off to its best advantage. It was about the clothes. Not about the girl.

"We don't have time for this. You're next. Go." He made a shoeing motion with his hand, not even looking at her.

Music blared in the background. The crowd outside was loud and boisterous. Earlier a big-name buyer had arrived unexpectedly and demanded a front row seat. That event had seemed to flip the switch from "normal" to "electric" and may even explain how she had been given an outfit she'd never even tried on.

Lights glared from the ceilings and reflected off the multitude of mirrors and the plain white walls. Models bustled around in various stages of undress. Assistants scurried after them, fixing broken straps, handing off last-minute replacement shoes or jewelry and adjusting the tiniest wrinkle.

It was true, to a certain extent, in this business one lost a lot of their modesty. One's body was just a background, the perfect background, hopefully, in which to showcase a designer's creations to their best possible angle.

But this see-through travesty that her handlers had put on her, unexpectedly and most definitely without her permission, was not something that she was going to let slide.

"I'm not wearing this."

Someone shouted her name. Sarwith, the top name facilitator who was backstage methodically, some would say even brutally, adjusting the clothes on models, to make sure the clothes were shown to the best advantage.

"You wear that. You're next." Sarwith's tall, slender blondness practically mirrored Morgan's own.

"It's see-through."

"It's perfect for your figure. When I saw you yesterday, I had to switch it for this show. Your body is the perfect canvas on which to display my handiwork." Her regal brows lowered. "No one else will do."

Henrique gave a last, quick tap to the barely-there top of the model he'd been working on. He straightened, and finally looked at her full-on. "Wear it. Or leave," he enunciated clearly. "And if you leave, don't think that you will ever work as a model again. Not in this town." Which happened to be New York. "And not in this business." He was only about five feet tall. She and Sarwith towered over him. Morgan's natural height of six feet one inch, was increased by the five inch, size twelve strappy heels she wore. "Not even a dogfood commercial."

Morgan stared at him. Really? After everything she'd done, everything she'd worked for, he'd seriously take it all away because of one see-through shirt?

Sarwith stood with her hands on her hips, a smug smile on her face, like she knew what Morgan would choose.

Surely Henrique wouldn't keep her from working. He couldn't do that.

But Henrique could. She didn't doubt it for a moment. Like everyone else in this business, he worked his fingers to the bone, but he had clout, and lots of it, especially when it came to models and recommendations.

Morgan was very aware that there were always younger, prettier, more slender models waiting in the wings for someone to fall. That had been her, not that long ago.

But she'd promised herself when she started that there were certain lines that she'd never cross. She'd never lain on anyone's couch, although she'd had the opportunity, and she'd watched as girls who walked into those certain offices and closed the door behind them had shot to super-stardom practically overnight.

She'd be lying if she said she'd never been tempted to take that route. Everyone did it.

But she'd turned those offers down. She'd had negative balances in her checkbook. She'd downgraded apartments and even been evicted over over-due rent. She'd scrimped and struggled, working as a waitress, a cashier, a body-double, anything. She'd take any job that would give her the flexibility to drop it and do a show at the last minute. She'd never turned down a show. And she'd always shown up and done her best.

It was finally paying off. For the last six months, her star had risen, and finally she was here, at New York Fashion week. Her years of struggle and having nothing were giving way to a gold mine. All she had to do was walk out that runway in the see-through shirt that she already wore. Thirty seconds. It would take thirty seconds. She'd already caught the eye of several designers, and her agent had spoken with her for over an hour last night after the practice. She was on the cusp of making it big. It had been her dream since her dorky, awkward, embarrassing teenaged years in her remote North Dakota high school.

With her thick glasses and nasty scaly, red skin along with years of acne, not to mention her height which had her towering over her teachers and classmates since she was thirteen, and hunching her shoulders and bending down to try to make herself smaller so she'd not stick out so dramatically, she'd never been considered a beauty.

It wasn't until she'd studied nutrition in college and started eating from the salad bar instead of chowing down on friend chicken and boxed pasta, quit watching tv and started exercising and, maybe the most dramatic changes – her braces had finally come off after four long years, and she'd gotten contacts.

Her body shape had changed. Her skin glowed with health. And, lo and behold, she'd attracted the attention of people who thought with a little hard work she could really make it as a model.

Because of growing up on a small ranch in North Dakota, hard work was something she was familiar with.

Multiple people were calling her name now. Henrique had his arms crossed, and his foot tapped. Other models and stylists had stopped to stare at the latest drama queen who was going to demand her way.

The pressure to give in and conform, to not throw away everything she'd gained, to do what was expected, was strong. These people didn't understand the values she'd been brought up with, and considered her refusal a power play. Or a temper tantrum.

This wasn't the first time she'd wondered why she'd worked so hard to be successful in an industry that had not time for morality, modesty or the values that related to those things.

Inside of her those two sides warred. One side begging her to conform, to give in and do what they wanted, to keep her position and garner prestige and be successful, showing everyone who'd ever called her ugly or fat that she'd won. Against the other side that pleaded with her to see the value in modesty and morality and to not allow the rest of the world to dictate right and wrong to her.

"Onstage. Now," Henrique barked.

She turned her back, walking to her station and putting her own clothes back on. Ignoring the shocked looks and the behind-the-hand whispers and several catty comments from her "friends," she picked up her purse and walked out of the room.

FORD IGNORED THE THUMPING pain in his head and the burning in his eye. He blinked, but didn't take his hands from his keyboard to rub it like his brain subconsciously urged him to do. He was close. Very close to getting the prototype dialed down to quality that was affordable to middle class Americans.

"Ford, I'm leaving."

And, just like that, the zone he was in vanished like a bubble on a windy day. He shoved back away from his desk in the darkened room

– all the rooms in his house were dark – and turned to the doorway where his sister, Georgia, stood. Her hair in wild disarray around her head, but what else was new, and a bag slung over her shoulder. That, unusual.

She'd taken amazing care of him over the last decade or so. Handling his moods – he knew he had moods – and making sure he ate, exercised, knew his calendar and appointments, and she even gave interviews in his stead. Because he wasn't taking his ravaged face into a studio. Nor was he giving interviews from his home. It was his sanctuary.

He'd quit college after the farming accident that had taken his leg and eye and two fingers, along with his handsome looks. But his self-confidence hadn't disappeared until Shauna had broken up with him. In the hospital. Two days after the accident.

She hadn't wanted to be shackled to someone she was "going to have to play nursemaid" to. Her words.

Bill Gates didn't have a college degree.

Ford snorted. He wasn't quite as successful as Bill Gates.

Yet.

"Fine. Leave."

Georgia put her hand on her hip. "You're not giving me a guilt trip about finally going to Europe like I've always dreamed about."

"No." He was, but technicalities.

"Morgan Nelson will be here later today. I wanted to have a few days to train my replacement, but you nixed every applicant I had until her."

He hadn't wanted anyone young or good-looking. He didn't even want middle-aged and good-looking. Basically, he wanted someone the rest of the world would not consider good-looking. Someone like him.

Georgia hadn't shown him Morgan's picture, but he remembered the Nelson's niece from school. She'd been a lot younger than him, but their schools were small, the Nelson's were fellow ranchers, and it was hard to forget Morgan. She'd been quiet. Shy. Although she seemed like a nice girl. His friends had described her as moldy dumpling with legs and glasses. They had never teased her personally, and he hadn't joined in the discussion, but thinking back, he knew her looks would not intimidate him.

"She's a North Dakota girl." He finally spoke since Georgia seemed to be waiting for him to say something. Normally he didn't appease her, but since she was leaving for four weeks, he made an exception. Mostly because there was a twinge in his chest that threatened to become loneliness after she walked out.

"She is. She's also quite smart and willing to learn and work hard. I've left detailed instructions, but Ford..."

She waited until Ford met her gaze.

"You're going to have to help her some. I can't explain to her in a note how to do everything that I do." She gave a humorless laugh. "I never know what you're going to have me doing when I get up in the morning."

That was true. Most of the time, he didn't know what the day was going to bring, either. The tech industry moved fast. Staying one step ahead could mean success. Staying well-ahead almost guaranteed success. He aimed to outpace it every day.

Too bad he couldn't get the one billion dollars he'd been willed from Mr. Edwards at Sweet Water Ranch. But he had to be married. No chance of that happening. Which was fine. He was already a self-made multi-millionaire. If he had the money, in the next year, he could be a multi-billionaire. Without the money, it would happen eventually. Just not as fast.

"Ford. Promise me you'll go easy on her. Be nice. Give her a chance."

He didn't say anything. But he would. He'd been voted best-looking and most likely to succeed in his small senior class. One of those were still true. Now, it was hard to be around beautiful, or even pretty, women. It made him too conscious of his own lack.

It wouldn't be hard to deal with dumpling girl. He wouldn't feel inferior. Maybe they'd understand each other. At the very least, she shouldn't be too put off by his face, since she'd dealt with the same issues as him, although she'd never had an accident.

He hated the bitterness in his thoughts. But that was a by-product of the accident too. Or maybe just a by-product of Shauna.

Whatever. Right now it didn't matter. Since his most loyal friend and companion, Georgia, was leaving him for four weeks.

"Ford." Georgia leveled her eyes at him. Her face got the stern, serious expression on it that he'd only seen a time or two. "If she quits, I'm not coming back."

He couldn't stop his reaction as his eye snapped to hers. Eye. He had an ugly, puckered scar where his right eye should have been. He used to wear an eye patch, but it was itchy and Georgia didn't care. Their housekeeper, Mrs. Torgerson, was in her early sixties. She, along with her husband, kept the house and grounds. Georgia was basically his personal assistant, face of his company and general all-around whatever he needed person. There was no way she could hire any one person to do what she did, but he'd resigned himself to the fact that he was going to have to deal for four weeks. But if Georgia didn't come back...

He searched her face. She was joking.

She crossed her arms over her chest. "Try me." She tapped her toe on the ground. That was Georgia. Never still. "If you hadn't dragged your feet and only given me permission to hire her last night, I could have trained her properly."

She lowered her eyes at him. "So of course she can't just rush over, but needs a little extra time to pack for *four weeks.*"

Georgia wasn't going to make him feel guilty. He wanted someone he could depend on. Not someone who was out ramming around. Like there was anything to do in rural North Dakota, anyway, but still, he wanted her available to him if he needed her, just like Georgia was.

Georgia sighed and walked into the room. "You're a good man, Ford." She knew his work went beyond the things that would make him money. "But you're being consumed with bitterness."

That wasn't anything he didn't know. He just didn't know what to do about it. He stood to meet her, his prothesis making it slightly difficult, even after more than a decade of practice. If he'd have been able to keep his knee joint, it would have been easier.

Georgia put her arms around his waist. Georgia was a huge pile of energy wrapped up in a tiny, almost-five-foot-tall bundle. He was almost a foot and a half taller than her. His height was about the only thing the accident hadn't stripped from him.

"I love you, Ford. You and Palmer were about the best big brothers a girl could have. But I can't save you from yourself."

He bent over, hugging her back. He knew she was right. He needed saved from himself. But he didn't know how or what he needed to do to even start. How did a man accept the fact that he would be ugly and alone for the rest of his life, and that all the money in the world would be cold comfort when he'd driven everyone who cared about him away?

THANKS FOR READING!

Click HERE[3] to order *Cowboys Don't Marry the Beauty*.

Reviews are welcome and appreciated!

Recipe!

Acapulco Chicken submitted by Linda Dreher
  2-3 chicken breasts, cooked and chopped
2 cans cream of chicken soup
small container sour cream
1 1/2 cups jack cheese
2 T flour
2 T butter or margarine
1 small onion diced about 1/2 a cup
1 small can diced green chilis or 1 medium jalapeño diced (from can)

Directions:

Cook and chop up chicken, set aside

In medium skillet, melt butter and add onions, sauté till transparent about 3 minutes.

Add flour, cook and stir about 2 minutes.

Add cream of chicken soup, sour cream, green chilis or jalapeños and 3/4 cup of the cheese, stir till all blended. Add chicken and stir together.

Spray a 9x9 baking dish with oil and add the mixture. Spread remaining cheese on top.

Bake at 375 for about 30 minutes or till top gets slightly brown. Put under broiler for a few minutes if you want a deeper brown top. Serve over rice of your choice.

My sister gave me the recipe many years ago, don't know where it came from before that.

The recipe is one of our families very favorite. This recipe is my youngest son's favorite recipe since he was very young. He is now 27 and also his birthday dinner request. We have it at least once a month.

You need to try it, it is so delicious and cheap to make for a lot of people. Enjoy! Linda